SMOKE

KRIS MICHAELS

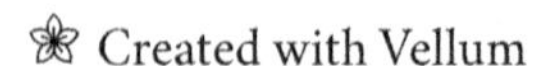
Created with Vellum

CHAPTER 1

"Stand by."

Charley snorted at Smoke's whispered command. Where the hell was she going to go? They were in the middle of the Caribbean, for God's sake. She planted her feet shoulder-width apart and moved with the roll of the yacht. Ribbons of orange, pink, and purple painted the sky as the sun started to dip in the west. Frustrated, she sighed, "Smoke, I don't see anything." Yet she continued to survey the horizon.

"Neither do I. Guardian, could you check your signal and validate our location in relation to your bogey?" Smoke's question was one she'd wanted to ask for the last twenty minutes. They should be able to *see* the ship by now.

"Hold on." Jewell's voice in her ear was also something she'd gotten used to since she'd started working with Smoke.

Although most of their recent assignments had been more about running her through her paces than working at a level Smoke was used to, she shouldn't really complain. She was in heaven. Well, actually, she was smack dab in the middle of a sexually frustrated limbo-type world that consisted of the ocean and Smoke. Which wasn't exactly heaven, but it wasn't a hardship, either.

Jewell's voice interrupted her thoughts. "I've refreshed everything. They are coming right at you. From the west, you have to be able to see them."

"Nope. Nada. Nothing." She didn't see shit.

"Guardian, there is just us and the gulls out here," Smoke added.

"They're coming straight for you," Jewell insisted.

"Charley, do you see anything? Aircraft, boat?" Smoke asked.

"Nothing," she replied again. There was silence for several minutes.

"You've got to be able to see it. Holy shit, it's going to ram you!"

Charley jumped at the stressed warning and did a quick three-sixty. Nothing but water as far as the eye could see. She swung her attention to the walk outside the bridge where Smoke was now positioned with binoculars. "There's nothing," she said to him, not Guardian, although Guardian could hear what they were saying.

"It is right on top of you." Jewell's voice hardened.

She scanned in a three-sixty arc. *No, the only thing out here are the clouds and the water.*

"There is nothing here, Guardian," Smoke repeated her thoughts.

"It.... shit... it just freaking passed *through* you, heading east. How in the hell?"

"Submarine," Smoke spoke and Charley raced to the other side of the ship. She stared at the darkening water.

"Did you see it?" She shielded her eyes and called up to her partner.

He shook his head, still staring at the water with his binoculars. "No, but it is the only explanation."

Bengal's voice came over the comms. "We're continuing to track the signal. Stand down for now, we'll contact you with further information. CCS clear."

Charley sighed and rolled her shoulders as the other entities that were on the comm loop signed out. Her nerves were on end. Guardian had been tracking this... blip... for days. A fucking submarine? She chuckled and then laughed. Of course, a fucking submarine. She wanted to punch something, or run, or God, have hot sex for hours.

She arched her back and stretched. Sex wouldn't happen, at least as long as she was assigned to Smoke as a partner. The assassin had put her firmly in the do not touch category. He gave her a wide berth and just about had a coronary every time she flirted with him. Which was a damn shame. Dan Collins was an identical likeness of his famous little brother Chris Collins, who was a box office phenom. Smoke was taller and he certainly had more muscle, but they shared that fucking sexy-as-hell smile and dark brown eyes rimmed with darker lashes that would rival the best mink false eyelashes in the world. There was no doubt why Chris had such success—just looking at either man was enough to ignite panties.

Blockbuster after blockbuster sprayed Chris'

face—and therefore, Dan's—all over the place. No wonder Smoke preferred to float out in the middle of nowhere. Even with the changes he'd made to his appearance, there was always someone who recognized or thought they recognized him. Seriously, both of the Collins brothers were *smoking* hot.

Charley chuffed out a frustrated laugh as she took the stairs down to the galley level. *Smoke was smoking hot.* With that thought, she wanted a drink and made a beeline to the bar. As she poured two fingers of a smokey bourbon, she chuckled again as her thoughts bounced and then… A blink preceded her laughter. She had Smoke on the mind. Or she had… The first chords of the song *Smoke on the Water* rolled through her mind and she sniggered before she tossed back the drink. Did *anyone* know how erotic that song was for her? No, probably not. Perhaps she needed a Smoke-abotomy. *Right... you are fucking losing your mind, girl.* Yep. Gonzo. Lord, excess energy coursed through her veins. She needed some way to burn away this sizzle under her skin. Sex would be her remedy of choice. Sex with Smoke.

The combustible tension between them had started as teasing on her part. The casual flirt because, hell yeah, the man singed her lady parts with a smile, drove her insane with his wink and laugh, and dear God, when the man stripped down to board shorts and nothing else, she was rendered speechless. The six weeks she'd certified as divemaster were where the tension really started, at least for her.

Roatan, Honduras was a tropical paradise personified. Crystal-clear water, white sand beaches, and a quiet, secluded southeast side where locals headed to avoid the tourists—and where Smoke put her through her paces for her divemaster certification. It was arduous and intensive as conducted, a complete water-skills assessment to include a SCUBA equipment change underwater. Those tests were followed by a diver rescue, dive skills, and practical application skills assessment before he performed not one but four practical tests on her abilities.

Physically exhausted each night, they did little but grab a sandwich and rest on the deck before they dragged themselves to their separate quarters and fell exhausted into bed. Smoke never opened up to her, his answers were closed and guarded, but occasionally, he would laugh and joke with her. It was obvious that, to Smoke, theirs was a student/teacher relationship, and *that* grated on her more each time he ignored her. The more he pulled away and fortified his defenses, the harder she'd pushed to try to knock them down. *So what? Was a little fun, flirty distraction a bad thing?*

Smoke sauntered into the lounge. She glanced up, and like a fly stuck to a long string of sticky paper, she didn't move. Well, her eyes did. Oh fuck, his muscled legs filled out the board shorts, pulling the material tight. He turned to go sit down and her eyes dropped down the perfect V of his back to the tight, high ass. She groaned under her breath and poured another drink. He rolled his shoulders, bringing her attention to their breadth and build.

He turned and glanced at her glass. "Pour me one, please?" Smoke slid onto one of the couches and dropped his head back to the cushions. The muscles of his neck corded in relief against his dark tan skin. *Shit.* She jolted and unfroze her muscles, turning her attention to the liquor in front of her. A generous splash of bourbon for her and one for him went into the tumblers. She walked over and dropped onto the other side of the couch after handing him his drink. Tucking into the corner of the couch, she boldly lifted her feet, dropping them on his leg. His muscles under her calves tightened immediately. Yes, he did notice her. These reactions weren't revulsion. *That* she knew for a fact. She hid her satisfaction at his response behind the rim of her drink.

Smoke pushed up into a sitting position, hiding the interest building behind his board shorts. She let her legs drop to the floor. Maybe she needed to up this little game of cat and mouse. "What should we do now?" She ran her finger around the rim of her crystal tumbler. "I'm bored."

Smoke's eyes narrowed as he looked at her. "Bored?" There was a hoarseness in his voice that she hadn't heard before.

She sighed and tipped her drink back, finishing it before she licked her lips and nodded. "Very. If only there was something to do way out here." She stood, sat her tumbler down, and slowly lifted off her t-shirt that covered the white and gold bikini top she was wearing.

Her hands moved to the button of her cut-off shorts when Smoke popped off the couch. "I need to… ah, check… something." He bolted, leaving his drink on the coffee table. If a cartoon cloud of dust could have followed him out the door, it would have.

Charley rolled her eyes heavenward and fell on

the couch. Damn, what did she have to do to get Smoke to drop whatever prude guidelines he was clutching as tight as an old woman clutched a string of pearls? She reached over and grabbed his glass. With a slight buzz overtaking her, she took another sip of his liquor. The bourbon wasn't bad. Granted, it wasn't Pappy Van Winkle's Family Reserve 20-year-old bourbon, but it wasn't rotgut either. She'd had both and preferred the Pappy, not that she'd ever tell anyone that. Well, no one around here at least. She took another sip and closed her eyes.

Sexually frustrated at twenty-two. Why did men act so weird? She needed to ask her mom that question the next time they talked. They were completely, utterly stupid animals at times. She wanted sex. For God's sake, how difficult was that concept to grasp? No strings attached. How hard could that be? Every man's dream, right? You'd think, but… nope. Not so with Smoke.

"Another dive test?" She pulled out the dive gear and started her inspection of her equipment. They'd traveled for four days to get to the northern Gulf Coast of the United States. He made her listen to and repeat the

correct procedures for tapping, wrapping, and strapping explosives in an underwater environment. She could recite the processes in her sleep, backward, and probably backward in her sleep, too.

"No. We're going to place underwater charges and take down that tower." He nodded to a hundred-foot tower on top of a sea-based platform. The platform surrounding the tower was probably a hundred-foot by a hundred-foot square.

She shielded her eyes and squinted toward the structure. "Hate to tell you this, but there are US Government signs all over that thing."

"Uncle Sam is the one who wants it down. The tower doesn't serve a purpose any longer."

"So, what do we do?"

"Today, you're going to tell me. You'll do a structural assessment dive first, come back up, and you'll build a plan and tell me exactly what we are going to do. You'll walk me through the smallest detail and then you'll do the job, with me watching, of course."

The day was a major thrill. Everything she'd learned from him during the last months became a laser focus of intent. She made the assessment dive and mapped out the tower. When they surfaced, she went to work. She determined the size of charge required and wrapped each explosive package, careful to follow what he'd taught her. She attached the cord, determined the length needed and what type of strapping would be required as well as the placement of each bundle.

Up on top, she attached the detonation device and took a deep breath before she looked over at Smoke. A smile as bright as the Caribbean sun sucked the air from her lungs. He nodded to the detonator. "Blow it."

She lifted the safety, pushed the button, and counted. One thousand - one. One thousand - two, and... A series of four explosions rumbled almost as one. She watched the water displace with each one and then heard the whine of metal bending as it collapsed and fell across the water. She watched, enthralled as the tower splashed in the exact direction she'd planned. When it fell under the water with a slap of waves covering it, she shouted in triumph and spun around. Smoke grabbed her and lifted her high in the air before setting her down with a whoop of ecstasy. She didn't think about it; she just toed up and kissed him. Fuck, he was delicious and as hungry for her as she was for him. Until he wasn't. He jerked away from her so fast that in a blink, he was five feet away.

"Congratulations. I'll report in." He was gone the next second.

She dropped her head back and stared at the darkening sky. The tiny connection of that kiss sparked a whirlpool of desire. But it was as plain as the nose on her face—Smoke wanted nothing to do with her. What a shame.

Charley shook off the need to revisit that wonderful evening and wandered out onto the deck and gazed out at the Caribbean sky. It was harder to stop thinking about than she would have liked. That little episode had happened about a month ago. She laughed at her embarrassing-as-fuck memories. "To sex, or the lack thereof!" She toasted the thin air and downed the rest of Smoke's bourbon. Tonight was a good night to get a little sloppy, go skinny dipping in the hot tub, and then maybe give herself a little satisfaction.

Geez... men. No, not men. Man. One sexy-as-hell man who was pissing her off. She'd climb him like a jungle gym and swing from his apparatus if he even so much as looked at her twice. Yeah, no, not Mr. Collins. The man was a saint. Saint Dan. She watched the last of the spectacular sunset. The last breath of another day. She toasted the glory with words her father had whispered to her mother countless times. "Today is over. May tomorrow bring us continued love and happiness."

The ship's engines roared to life and she heard the anchor being winched up. Smoke was obviously making for port. Well, good. She could find something or *someone* to do on dry land. Her options were... limitless. She dropped into one of the chairs on the deck and watched the disturbed water trail behind the powerful motors of the boat as they plowed through the ocean.

She needed to stop drinking. There was no way Smoke could dock the boat without her help and falling between the boat and the dock was a great way to break her neck. Damn it. She glanced up and caught a shooting star. She closed her eyes and made a wish. One that she knew would never come true, but it had been her wish for as long as she could remember. A sad smile pulled across her lips. Any day now, her world could implode, and because of that, she was going to live it to the max. If Smoke didn't want anything to do with her, so be it. She'd find someone else with whom to celebrate her temporary freedom.

Smoke stood at the captain's console and stared out at the darkening water. He waited as the operator switched him through to the Rose.

"What is it this time? Did your boat blow up?" Fury's voice cracked over the connection.

"It's a ship and no."

Fury sighed, "Have you been stabbed, shot, or mortally injured?"

"No. Who is she?" He needed to know. He knew she was someone important. The contextual clues were all over the place, but no one—absolutely no one—was talking to him, and *that* was more concerning than the mystery surrounding Charley.

"Your partner. End of story."

"That's not the end of the story. Hell, I don't even think that's the beginning of the story. Who. Is. She?"

"Why?" Fury drawled the word.

"Because I'm going insane."

"And? How is that different from your mental attitude every day?"

The disinterest in Fury's voice launched his eye roll. "Dude, let me put this as delicately as I can. She wants... a relationship. A physical relationship!"

"For the record, I one hundred percent don't recommend it. I fucking don't approve, you're too old for her, but Guardian doesn't have a policy against fraternization."

"I'm going fucking insane. Except for a few days before the holidays, we've been on this yacht together. Alone. All day, all night. Every day. Every night." His fist grabbed the wheel hard enough to leave fingerprints in the metal. "Look, I've been accused of being a manwhore, but we both know I'm not. I don't jump into bed with just anyone. She's..." *God, she's like a breath of fucking fresh air. Irreverent and impossible.* Sexy, young, beautiful, the adjectives could go on forever.

"What the fuck do you want from me, man? She's over twenty-one. She's a trained operative."

"But she's someone important, isn't she?"

"She is important to important people, yes," Fury finally acknowledged the fact.

"Yeah, so I can't go there." He was the odd one out at every level. He was a Shadow but wasn't really. His assignments usually supported other Shadows; it was rare he had a mission without interacting with one of them. He'd even gotten to know the new generation of Shadows in that capacity. No interaction since he'd taken Charley on as a partner, though, which in itself was telling.

"Don't let it affect your teamwork and you'll be fine."

"Speaking of teamwork..."

Fury knew what he was talking about and responded immediately, "Sage hasn't made contact with me yet. Listen, no offense... Well, fuck that, take offense if you want, but you need to start focusing on the future, not the past. The man has things to take care of. If and when he contacts me, I'll let you know. I already told you that. He knows your number. If he needs to talk, he'll call you."

"Yeah."

"Do you love him?" Smoke blinked at the question, but he didn't expect anything less from Fury. He was never one to beat around the bushes. Yeah, Fury knew he was bisexual, and he didn't give a flying fuck.

"It's not like that, man. He's like the little brother I never had."

"You *have* a little brother, shithead."

"I barely know Chris. He's lived in California with them since..." Smoke drew a deep breath; he wasn't going there. "...from the time Chris was five. He was groomed to be an actor from day one."

Unlike him. He was a huge disappointment to his mother and father who were barely "C" list actors that couldn't even sniff the Hollywood "B" list, but they had motivation and looks, which made two beautiful boys. Except he was defective and not a cash cow like Chris. He glanced at all the gauges on the console. He knew what each was, what they meant, and what they controlled, but he couldn't read a damn word without sounding each out like a preschooler. Severe dyslexia had made him unusable to his parents. A throwaway child that they had shoved in a group home and abandoned. Fuck, what were he and Fury talking about? Oh, right. "Sage needed my help."

"You taught him to sign. I'm confused about that. Why isn't sign language difficult for you?"

"I guess my brain processes it differently. The hand symbols aren't backward or fucked up. I can sign without a problem as long as I don't have to finger spell, and I was able to teach him. He's so damn smart. People treat him like an idiot because he stutters and it pisses me off." Sage knew his dirty little secret and they had an understanding. Neither was less for their disabilities, and that understanding deepened their relationship. Sage was his brother by choice, not blood, and Smoke was going insane not knowing how he was doing, but he'd promised Sage he'd let the man handle the situation on his own.

Smoke saw the lights of an island off to his right and checked his compass. Even with the fucked-up way his brain saw the letters, he knew how to read his gauge. Sage had marked north with a sharpie. A small dot that no one would notice, but it was there, just in case he got confused. Put N, S, E, and W into a written word and he was so screwed, but he adapted. He always did.

There was a long pause as he crawled out of the hole his disability sent him down. Finally, Fury replied, "Charley is connected in a major fucking way to people important to me, but she's her *own* woman. That is something you can take to the bank. Stop overthinking it."

"Yeah, easy for you to say that. You're not the one who's been sidelined with her as a partner."

This time the pause was weighty and heavy. "I'm not the one throttling you back. Take care of yourself and keep her from getting dead. I'd take it as a personal favor." The connection ended.

Smoke hung up. "Not getting dead is priority number one."

~

"Jewell, the floor is yours, bring all the others up to speed." Jason sat down in the secure conference room and took a mental roll call. Jacob, Tori, Anubis, and Joseph on video link, and Jewell and Bengal at the end of the table.

"Okay. For several months now, we've been monitoring chatter on the dark web. There is an American citizen working with the North Koreans."

Jacob cussed under his breath and leaned back in his chair. Tori placed her hand on his thigh and Jacob covered her hand.

Jewell brought her attention up to Jason and he nodded, giving her permission to continue. "His name is Darryl Clayborne, or it was. Darryl Clayborne ceased to exist four years ago. His digital footprint just evaporated."

"So, how did you identify that this guy in fact is in North Korea?" Tori leaned forward to see around Zane.

"Oh, that was Zane's idea. We accessed the security footage for all major points of entry and exit starting the week before the man disappeared."

"Who keeps security footage that long?" Jacob asked nobody in particular.

"Department of Homeland Security," Jewell, Zane, and Fury answered at the same time.

Jewell continued, "We identified him going out of the country and boarding a plane to Seoul, South Korea. From Seoul, he flew to Pyongyang, North Korea."

"Okay, but why are we tracking this guy? He can't legally go to North Korea without a special validation from the Department of State. Stupid fuck cut all ties with that move. Why would he want to do that?" Jacob gave Jason a quizzical look.

"I can answer that," Anubis chimed in. "With your permission, sir?"

Jason nodded. "Permission granted."

"Darryl Clayborne was once a Guardian Shadow recruit. He was an exceptional recruit but asked to be released from the training program. At the three-month point declared he couldn't continue and asked to be returned to serve out his prison sentence. As you know, at that point he knew nothing about us other than we were a private entity. We returned him to serve out his sentence. He escaped ten years later by viciously murdering three guards and two innocent bystanders as he was being taken to his annual parole hearing." Anubis cleared his throat. "From the information Jewell and her team have been able to gather, we believe Darryl Clayborne is recruiting and training assassins for North Korea."

Jacob shook his head. "Holy fuck. He saw the beginning of our system and copied it."

Anubis nodded. "But he only saw the very beginning of the training program. He hadn't made it to his substantive mental health evaluation. There was only physical and weapons training that Guardian uses to separate the wheat from the chaff. Clayborne, in our opinion, could have gone to the next level, but..."

"So, he's training assassins for North Korea?" Fury asked the question.

"Yes, but we believe he's also freelancing with those operatives." Jewell hit a few buttons and three pictures appeared on the video screen next to Anubis and Joseph. She continued, "Three victims that we can link via chatter to Clayborne's people. English, Italian, and American nationals. All three were assassinated, and the assassin taking credit is Akuma."

"Where have I heard that name?" Jacob swung his attention from the screen to Tori.

Fury sighed, "Shit. That's the name of the assassin Tempest said had taken a retainer to go after the Fates' killers."

"We believe Akuma is the codename used by a group of assassins who work directly for Clayborne. The murders of the Italian and American nationals were continents apart and the assassinations happened within minutes of each other."

"All right, is he coded?" Fury asked and looked directly at Jason.

Jason leaned forward and linked his fingers. Of all the operations he'd overseen in the years since he'd taken over Guardian, this one was fluid as water, and they were working in the dark. Literally. "He has been coded for human rights violations and atrocities that would make the Fates look like sweethearts."

Every eye tracked his direction. He took off his glasses and rubbed the bridge of his nose as he spoke, "I'm not at liberty to detail the information, but what is happening in that country to the North Korean people is sickening. Clayborne has blood on his hands. A lot of blood."

"Okay, so, if he is a ghost, how are we going to find him?" Tori asked.

"Oh, I can answer that one! His pocket watches." Jewell smiled. "He has a slight addiction. We know that from his intake forms when he was in our training system. Compliments of Mr. Xavier, we were able to put several watches up for auction in the last year. All have nanotech inserted into the workings behind the gears. Anyone who collects one of those watches would never disturb the mechanics." She smiled at Zane. "One of them, purchased by an online bidder, traveled to Nampo, a city just outside Pyongyang, located in South Pyongan Province. It is considered a special city within a city; it is also a water port for the country, one of the smaller ones, but it has egress methods the other cities don't."

"You believe that watch was purchased by Clayborne." Tori nodded, following the dots.

"I do. The other watches went to residences of wealthy collectors, known personnel."

Jason took over the conversation again. "Which brings us to the events of today. We have been tracking the watch and we believed Clayborne was on a ship in the Caribbean. There has been zero luck in obtaining an ID on Clayborne. We had an asset set up to ID the mode of travel. However, Clayborne was not on a boat, he was in a submarine."

"You're fucking joking?" Jacob looked from him to Joseph, to Anubis, to Jewell. "Shit."

"Do you know where the watch went?"

"We do, and we will be engaging; however, our problem is we don't know what Clayborne looks like now."

Fury spoke up, "Excuse me, how is that possible?"

"We followed the signal of the watch. Here, in the airport in Seoul, South Korea, was our first chance to confirm his identity. We have video of each person who entered that facility at the time Clayborne was there. None of them ticked on the facial recognition programs."

"He had plastic surgery," Tori spoke almost to herself.

"And he could be any one of over a thousand people who entered that terminal. The watch went to Singapore and disembarked. As you can imagine, we weren't able to get any video from them." Jewell cleared her throat. "He hopped from port to port in countries that we don't have reciprocal agreements with, of course. I'm told hacking into communist countries' databases is a bad thing." She stared directly at her husband, who lifted an eyebrow but remained silent.

Jacob chuffed, "Smart bastard."

"Who? Zane or Clayborne?" Anubis quipped.

"Both, but I was talking about Clayborne," Jacob clarified.

"He is. Off the charts smart," Fury agreed.

"So, what is Guardian's play? Bottom line?" Jacob looked at him.

"We identify Clayborne and take him out. But until we have a one hundred percent ID on the bastard, we are on a hold."

"You want us to fucking process his DNA before we take him out?" Fury's frustrated growl rang clearly in the room.

Jason lifted his eyes to his older brother. "If that is what it takes, yes. We are not working outside the restrictions that were placed on this folio. Get Smoke to where that watch docked. Send him the address and have them conduct surveillance. They are not to engage. Copy?"

Fury sighed and nodded. "You're going to have to take off the training wheels sometime."

"Surveillance only at this point."

"Roger that. The Rose is out." Joseph's picture disappeared.

"Training wheels?" Jacob looked from him to Anubis.

Anubis shrugged. “Not my story to tell.”

“Thank you for that,” Jason chuffed. “So, we are monitoring the location of the watch and we are awaiting surveillance photos, but this has the possibility of moving fast. Jacob, what teams do you have in the southeast?”

“Sierra, Tango, and Whiskey.” He glanced at Tori. “Missions in the southeast?”

“Several smaller ones, but we can pull one team and put them on standby.” Tori nodded.

“No need to pull them off missions yet. Anubis, is your asset in place?”

“Yes, sir. The asset arrived in the area yesterday. I'm adjusting positioning based on Jewell's latest input.”

“Good. Our chessboard is set, Clayborne moves first.” Jason picked up his tablet.

“You are aware that statistically speaking, the piece that moves first usually wins in the game of chess.” Jewell's voice stopped him halfway up from the chair.

Jason straightened and put on his glasses. “If we play fair, yes. We have more than a few tricks up our sleeves. Clayborne may be smart, but he isn't a Guardian. He isn't elite, and he isn't going to win. You have your assignments; this meeting is over.”

CHAPTER 2

Smoke piloted the ship into position and checked the depth finder before he dropped anchor.

"We aren't docking?" Charley's voice behind him instinctively tightened his muscles. Which was his defensive reaction toward her, and it had been his default lately, which sucked because she was a damn good kid. *Kid*. Fuck, he hadn't thought about her as a *kid* in a long, long time. She was all woman.

He shook his head, clearing it and honestly trying to remember what question she'd asked him. Docking. That was it. "No." He turned and handed her the binoculars that were on the console next to him. "Three residences along that cliff. Second one from the right. That's where the signal is originating."

"What are we going to do from out here? I can barely make out the separation of the houses."

Charley lifted the binoculars to her eyes, which allowed him to stare at her. Her high cheekbones, full lips, and soft blush were mesmerizing. She dropped the binoculars and stared at him. Fuck, what had she asked? Oh. "We're out here until tomorrow night. Then we take a swim and do some surveillance."

A wide smile spread across her face. "Yes! Finally, something to do. I can't wait to swim until I'm exhausted. I'll check the tanks and equipment first thing in the morning."

He nodded. He loved the idea of a long swim, too. They'd move in closer to the shore after dark so they'd have enough air to make it to the coastline and back, but they both needed to get off the damn ship. Him for his sanity and for Charley... Well, she was young. Too damn young to be in this business, but that was his opinion, not Guardian's.

"Hungry?" She put the covers on the lenses of the binoculars and sat them down.

Starving, but not for food. "I could eat." Smoke

nodded to the secondary panel. "Deploy the sensors? I'll go see what I can scrounge up in the galley."

"Ah, no. You deploy the sensors and I'll go find something. I so do not want another sandwich."

"Hey, they're my specialty!" He grabbed his chest in mock horror.

"They are good, too. The first hundred or so times." She laughed and slapped his arm as she moved past. "Dinner consists of a protein, a veg, and a starch."

"But you get that with a sandwich," he called after her. At her laugh, he moved to the secondary panel, and from memory of the pattern started to deploy the sensors that would let him know if anything other than fish ventured near the ship.

He busied himself with the routine of bedding down his ship, checking the generators and the freshwater tanks along with the grey tank status. They'd need to dock in a week or so. With just two of them on the ship, they never ran low on water or generator fuel. He made his way up from the engine room to the galley. The aroma of something delectable brought his stomach to life with a loud rumble.

He leaned against the galley door and took in

the view. Charley had wrapped her hair into a messy bun on the top of her head. Her t-shirt was off, and she was wearing one of her many bikini tops; tonight, it was the white and gold one that showed off her tan. She had her back to him and was dancing with a spatula in one hand and a bottle of water in the other. She was singing a song from *Rent*. He'd watched that Broadway show a few years ago. It was fantastic. She shimmied her tight ass and sang without inhibition. She was damn good, too. At the chorus, he joined her. She jumped and spun, but he continued to sing. It took a couple of seconds, but she started to sing again. She turned and flipped the fish fillets she was pan frying as they sang the second verse and the chorus. He pulled dishes and silverware out and placed them on a tray to take to the table.

"You're good," Charley said when they finished the song.

"I can carry a tune. You're the one who is good. You nailed that high note." He took the tray out to the table and she followed with their full plates.

"Fish, rice, and salad." She set his plate in front of him.

"Thank you, it smells delicious."

"I hope so after I trashed your sandwiches." Charley sat down and smiled at him.

"Right? So rude." He smiled as he attacked the grouper. His eyes rolled back in his head when the explosion of flavor hit his tongue. "This is amazing."

"Thank you," Charley said before she took a bite. "Can I ask you something?"

He closed an eye and stared at her. "That's a loaded question."

She shot him a quick look. "How so?"

"If I say no, I'm being a shit partner. If I say yes, you'll pop off with a personal question that I'm not going to be inclined to answer." Smoke laid his fork down. "But bring it." He crossed his arms over his chest and gave her his attention.

"I've been going over the placement of the explosive component for land-based targets. Now, structurally, where would you put the first blast, and would you implode all vectors at the same time or vary the timers?" Charley took a drink of her water and stared at him.

Well. Damn. That was not the way he thought the conversation was going to go. "Personal preference only, I'd blow them all in a sequence of two-second spacing. Two seconds would give time for the initial outward blast, but not the implosion. If you waited any longer than that, the implosion may send debris to the next explosion site and take out the second, third, or fourth explosions."

"Wouldn't the explosions interfere with the triggering mechanisms?" Charley stabbed a forkful of salad as she asked.

"Not necessarily. There is new tech coming out all the time, but I stick with tried-and-true methods. Wireless phones are a fantastic trigger, cheap, and unless you deactivate the phone, you've got a reliable electric charge from the lithium batteries. Tell me what the phone's weakness is in this situation."

He took a bite of his fish as she finished her salad. She wiped her lips before she spoke, "Cell phones can be jammed, but that could happen to a remote wireless, too, right?"

"It *could* if the frequencies are known. Remember, cell phones operate in a set range of frequencies. They are governed by law, so you can program a jamming device to that specific range."

"So, while cells are convenient, they can be defeated."

He nodded. "If someone suspects you're rigging an explosion, yes." He took another bite of food. The seasoning was amazing, way better than a freaking sandwich. "Remote triggering, as in wireless signals to a terminal, isn't a long-distance winner. Cell phones beat wireless transmissions thanks to the proliferation of the cell towers, but if you are working against a known entity and you have a safe place to trigger a wireless explosion, they are exceptionally reliable."

"More than timers?"

"I don't like timers as a rule. Too many variables can come into play."

"Such as?"

"Innocents. Timers can't be deactivated. If an innocent wanders into your zone of destruction, you've taken out noncombatants. Not our goal." He took a drink of his water. "I've been at this business for most of my adult life. We take out specific targets, that's the mandate. Timers are messy. I'll only use them if there is no chance of collateral damage."

"Such as taking out a ship at sea." She glanced up at him between bites. "Is that why you deploy the sensors every time we stop?"

"Absolutely. That and this is my home. I consider dropping those sensors like a house alarm."

She chuckled. "ADT at sea."

"Exactly."

"Okay, in your opinion, what's the most reliable triggering mechanism for a land-based structure?"

"Hard wired, baby. That's the most reliable but also takes the most time. You need absolute cover while you're working, and this method is the way that will get you killed the fastest. Even a moron can follow a wire to its source."

She chuckled. "Find a lot of morons in this line of work?"

"More than you could possibly imagine." Smoke put down his fork and leaned on his forearms. "I was working an operation for Guardian. A Russian crew scuttled their ship because the navigation system went crazy. They entered US waters because they couldn't steer the damn thing. Needless to say, that didn't go over well with Mother Russia. They were told to sink their own damn ship so the Americans couldn't board them and get their tech. They were damn close to the coast of Florida when they sank her."

Charley's dark brown eyes grew large. "You were told to blow it up?"

"After a dive crew salvaged damn near every system. Water doesn't destroy configurations, and agencies gained serious intel from the hardware alone. Anyway, I was rigging the thing so the Russians wouldn't ever be able to know what was recovered. I had it laced and rigged. Of course, up above, I had my dive flag up on my ship. I don't want some random pleasure boat to be the reason I end up dead, you know?"

Charley leaned back and chuckled. "I can see where that would be a motivational reason to fly the dive flag."

"Right? Anyway, I'm getting back on my old boat. I have miles of det cord and I'm going to get clear, right? Some rando ship shows up. They're having an orgy on the back deck. I mean there were naked people everywhere. They see me, and of course, they think I'm Chris."

Charley leaned in. "Oh shit. What happened?"

"People jumped off that ship and started swimming over to mine. We're talking fifteen, twenty naked people swimming across the open ocean, and I'm ready to blow this Russian boat into tiny pieces."

"How in the hell did you get them to leave?"

"I shouted 'shark' and contacted Guardian."

"Did it work?"

He laughed and shook his head. "The memory of all those drunk, naked people hustling it back to their yacht… Damn, it was freaking hilarious."

"What did Guardian do?"

"Called in the cavalry, but one very determined lady jumped back into the water after about twenty minutes of everyone looking for the shark that never was. She made it about three-quarters of the way to my ship, calling Chris' name about every hundred yards or so, screaming "I'm coming, I'm coming!" If it wasn't so pathetic it would be hilarious. Anyway, a Coast Guard cutter that had been on standby arrived and plucked her out of the water. Naked as the day she was born. They chased the boat out of the way and Guardian had the Coast Guard act as cordon until I was able to blow the hell out of the Russians' ship."

Charley laughed and settled back into her chair. She got quiet and then said, "That really must suck."

He knew what she was talking about, but he didn't want to go there. "Nah, I love blowing things up."

"Not what I meant." She stared straight at him.

He sighed; he knew she meant being mistaken for Chris. "It isn't great." Every man or woman that he'd ever dated had commented on the fact he looked like Chris Collins.

"I've met him, you know, your brother." She twirled her half-empty water bottle between two fingers on the table.

"Really? Let me guess, you found him irresistible." Of course, she did. Everyone loved Chris.

"You want the truth, or you want me to be nice?"

"Hit me with the truth." He was used to hearing how wonderful his brother was.

"The man is vain and shallow. His conversation centered on one thing and one thing only. Himself." She shrugged. "I couldn't see myself having an intelligent conversation with him or singing show tunes in the kitchen as I cook dinner. If he was a woman, I'd call him a vapid narcissist. He thinks *he's* the most interesting topic on the planet."

Smoke blinked several times. That was the first time his opinion of his brother had ever been voiced by someone other than himself. Not sure how to deal with her opinion, he joked,

"Well, tell me how you really feel, why don't you?"

"You don't want that." Charley stood and reached for the tray to clear the table.

He reached out and put a hand on her arm. She froze under his touch. "Tell me, please."

She released the tray and sat down, her warm skin sliding from his touch. "You want to know how I really feel?"

No. Yes. Hell, probably not. "I do."

Her eyes lifted to his. "I want you. You know I do. But it is more than that, more than a physical attraction, and not because of who your insipid brother is, but because of *who. You. Are.* You hide behind humor instead of having to deal with a family history that I have no doubt would make me mad enough to use the land-based explosive techniques we've been going over."

He swallowed hard and asked, "Who are you?"

"Who are you?" she countered immediately.

He narrowed his eyes. "You know who I am."

"No, *I don't.* I know who you let me see. What have you *ever* told me about yourself? What have you ever confided in me? How many conversations have we had that were deeper than your instruction or comments about the weather? We've been working and living together on this ship *alone,* for months, and we are no closer than strangers passing at a supermarket. You've held me at arm's length. You haven't allowed me to get close to you nor have you tried to get close to me. I'm tired of dancing this dance. I'll contact Fury and tell him to find you a new partner stat. This isn't working out." She stood and turned to leave.

He pushed back his chair and stood, asking again, "Who are you?"

She spun and yelled at him, "Why do you even care?"

"Because I..." How in the hell did he tell her that she was, in one way or another, almost constantly on his mind? That her presence on this ship had made the last months more than bearable and that was five thousand percent better than he thought they could be? That she was beautiful, both inside and out, and he'd take her to bed in a nanosecond if he could trust himself not to fuck up and hurt her?

"Right, just what I thought." She spun around again.

"Stop." He ground the word out.

Charley flounced around and put her hands on her hips. "Why?"

He stalked over to where she was. He opened his mouth to speak, but of course, the only thing he could say was, "Who are you?"

She lifted her chin and stared at him as she spoke, "The question you need to ask yourself is *why* do you care? Why is it important? I am a woman, a trained operative, and I have proven myself over and over to you, and yet you act as if I'm a piece of gum stuck to the bottom of your shoe."

He had, but not for the reasons she thought. But he went down the lane his stupid brain had chosen and demanded. "Answer my questions."

She shook her head. "No."

"Why not?"

"You don't trust me with your secrets, why should I trust you with mine?" She dropped her arms and sighed as if she were suddenly exhausted. "Goodnight. I'll see you in the morning." She stepped back from him one step and then another. Finally, she turned and walked down the hall toward her stateroom.

He dragged his hands through his hair that was too long and not its natural color. "Fuck!" He kicked the air and headed back to the table.

Looked like he had KP duty and more frustrations than answers.

He turned around and yelled down the hall, "Who the fuck are you?" His voice reverberated around the confines of the lounge. He muttered to himself as he loaded the dishes to the tray, "The President doesn't have any kids. Vice President?" He lifted his head and stared at the ceiling for a moment. "Nope, boys, five boys to be exact. Does the Chairman of the Joint Chiefs have kids? I'll have to ask Siri that shit. Who else would be so important that Fury and Anubis would hogtie me and put me on these benign ops?"

He made his way back into the kitchen and stopped as it all clicked into place. "Shit." He dropped the tray to the stainless-steel counter and put his hands on his hips. "She's a fucking *King*." That's it. It had to be. *Son of a bitch, why in the hell couldn't Fury just have said something? A personal favor. Fucker. Telling me without telling me.*

He smacked his head with an open hand. "Stupid. A King. Of fucking course. That explains everything. Yeah, screw this up and you'll piss off the entire family." He slammed the frying pan into the sink.

Hot water streamed into the pan as he recalled

each of the Kings and their position of power. Holy hell. Well, if they wanted him to babysit, they should have fucking told him. He dipped the sponge into the water and got it soapy. They had told him, hadn't they? No, not with words, but with the non-missions. Son of a bitch. He was growling at a stubborn piece of fish that was stuck to the frying pan when his cell phone went off.

Flinging suds off his hand, he reached into his board shorts and pulled out his phone, ready to lay into whoever was calling him this time. But Sage's number flashed across the screen. He scrambled to answer it, dropping it in the sudsy water in the process. He fished it out and wrapped it in a towel, drying it. Swiping the face, he yelled, "Sage?"

"W-whoa, you o-okay?"

He backed up and leaned against the refrigerator, sliding down it to sit on the floor. "Fuck, man, how the hell have you been? Are you ready to come back?"

"Okay. N-not y-yet. Things g-good t-there?"

"God, they saddled me with a babysitting project. I just figured out she's a freaking King."

"W-what?" There was humor in Sage's voice. The bastard was loving this.

"Oh, screw you, man. Let me fluff it out so you

can laugh some more. She's about five-ten, legs that go to the moon and back, a rocking hard body, she's a trained operative, now a certified divemaster, *and* she likes explosives."

"She's p-perfect for y-you."

"Right? Did I mention she is just over legal?"

"And?"

"And what? A King, and she's twenty-two years old!"

Sage laughed, "A-and? A-are they g-going t-to take away y-your b-birthday if you h-hook up with her?"

"She's a fucking King!"

Sage dissolved into laughter. Smoke ran his wet hand through his hair and started to laugh, too.

"G-go f-for it. Be h-happy. M-molehill."

"A molehill and not a mountain, huh?" Well, maybe he'd been blowing the fact that she was a King up just a bit, but still…

Sage gave a hum of agreement.

"How's things going there, Sage? You could have called, man. I've been worried sick."

"S-sorry. Not a good p-place, y-you know?"

He sighed. They'd talked about Sage's folks and his upbringing. "Yeah, and that's why I was worried, man. You don't have to stay there. Come back to Guardian."

"C-can't. N-not y-yet."

"But you will come back, right?" The silence on the other end of the phone forced him to look at his to make sure it hadn't fritzed out because of the dip in the suds, but they were still connected. "Sage, talk to me man."

"Y-you t-tell her?"

"No."

"F-fuck. Open up, d-damn it. T-take a f-f-f damn ch-chance."

"I will if you promise me you'll come back to Guardian when whatever is happening at home is done."

"I-I'll try. Best I-I can d-do." Sage wouldn't lie to him and he wasn't the type to sugarcoat anything either.

"I'll take that. Don't let that place or those people get to you. You matter to me. You matter to Guardian. Those fuckers don't know what an asset you are, they don't know *who* you are. Do not let them suck you back into a life you don't want to live. Promise me."

"G-got to go. W-whatever it t-takes."

"You remember that Sage. For as long as it

takes. One call and I'm heading your way. One call. One word. I've got your back. I'll always have it, you know that right?"

"Y-yeah. I do. L-let her in, D-Dan."

The connection died, and Smoke dropped his phone on the floor. He dropped his head back against the fridge. "What a fucking day."

CHAPTER 3

Charley pulled the last of the oxygen tanks from the shelving units and hauled them over to the workspace under the overhang of the main floor of the yacht. The shade kept the area cool and the ever-present breeze ventilated the small area. She inspected each piece of their SCUBA equipment, following the checklist carefully. There were things she'd play fast and easy with but safety wasn't one of them. Especially since she was pissed enough to strangle Dan. As soon as she finished the safety check, she was heading to the bridge and making that call to Joseph. She'd never once mentioned her connection to him or anyone at Guardian, and she sure as hell didn't want to use that card now, but Smoke obviously didn't trust her. Hell, for that matter, with all the shit gopher jobs he'd been assigning them, it was pretty fucking obvious that *Joseph* didn't trust her, and *that...* Well, *that* pissed her off. She cussed under her breath, dropping a string of words that would singe the hair on Beelzebub's ass.

The low hum of an outboard motor pulled her up from her crouched position, but her mumbled rant continued until she realized the boat was on a direct course toward them. She made a quick sweep of the area. No weapons that were visible. Her nine mil was just on the other side of the exterior wall which shielded it from view. She pulled her t-shirt off and shimmied out of her cut-offs. She grabbed a bottle of sunscreen and started slathering on the greasy mess. She needed to look like a tourist, not a deckhand. Thanks to her large silver aviators, she could watch the upcoming boat without them knowing it. When it slowed, she lifted from where she'd perched herself like a paid advertisement for cocoa butter. The driver of the boat waved and called out, "Ahoy!"

It was everything she could do not to laugh out loud at the dick. *Seriously, how fucking cheesy was that?*

"Ahoy, can we help you?" Charley heard Smoke's response before she saw him. He had stripped down as well. Fuck, the man was a walking wet dream. He wore his baseball cap and aviators, and the distance between the two vessels would help to obscure his likeness to his brother.

"We're looking for a small craft that didn't come into harbor last night. How long have you been here?" The man shielded his eyes as he called across the water, maneuvering his smaller boat alongside the yacht.

"Since last night," Smoke answered and casually walked behind her, obscuring the driver's view of him a bit more.

"What kind of craft are you looking for?" Charley sauntered forward, keeping herself between Smoke and the boat pilot.

"Small craft. Twelve-foot skiff. A couple of locals went fishing and didn't come back."

Charley continued to rub the suntan lotion on her skin but answered, "We haven't seen anyone. Have we, honey?"

Smoke shook his head. "Sorry, not a soul out here except us and now you."

The man lifted his chin. "Getting ready to go diving?"

"No, just cleaning the equipment and getting it ready for the next time we want to use it. Are you with the Grand Cayman Coast Guard? Do you have a number we can call if we see the skiff?" Charley braced her arm against the exterior wall of the yacht and leaned against it in a completely casual pose, but her hand was now near her weapon. Smoke came up behind her and put his hand on her hip possessively.

"No, just helping out. If you find any indication of that skiff, you can call it in on the radio." The man gave them a wave and pulled away from the yacht.

"That was weird." Charley stepped away from Smoke, dislodging his hot palm from her hip.

"I've been monitoring radio traffic this morning. There hasn't been any chatter of a missing fishing craft." Smoke stared at the speedboat as it headed away from the ship. The man's tan skin hugged the swells of his back. Charley pushed her attention past the man in front of her to the boat that was disappearing toward the island.

"So, my statement stands. Weird." She pulled on her shirt and stepped back into her shorts, fastening them quickly. "The equipment is ready to go." She turned away from him, speaking over her shoulder. "I'm using the secure comms to call the Rose."

"Charley, wait. Before you call your… Joseph, let's finish the mission."

She stopped three steps up and looked back at him. "You mean the surveillance. We haven't had a real mission since I stepped foot on this ship."

"I'm no happier about that than you are."

"So, it's Joseph."

"He said he wasn't the one throttling us." Smoke sat down on a fixed storage container. "Look, I admit I've been less than forthcoming in the past months."

The indignant snort that resonated from her was all the agreement he was going to get.

He chuckled and shook his head. "But you haven't been either."

She placed both hands on her hips and glared at him.

He sighed, "All right, all right. How about we start over?"

"You want me to call you Gramps again?"

A bark of laughter came back at her. "You do that, and I'll turn you over my knee and spank you."

A lightning bolt of desire lanced to her soul.

She cocked her head and narrowed her eyes at him. "Don't threaten me with a good time."

She watched it happen. His eyes darkened and he swallowed hard before he rolled his shoulders and drew a deep breath. "You into that?"

"No, but I'm into *you*. I've told you that in every way I know how. I'm not asking for a wedding ring or, hell, even exclusivity." She threw that last part in to ease his mind. She knew his reputation which, quite frankly, made his constant rebuffs that much harder to absorb, but the small flinch she saw when she said the words though... That was curious. Almost as if he didn't like that particular carrot.

He turned around and shoved his hands into his board short pockets. "I'm not into sleeping around." She remained quiet and he glanced over his shoulder at her. "I know what people say, but that shit's not true. I don't sleep around. I watched people shuffle through one-night stands my entire life. I can't..."

She closed her eyes and took a deep breath. *At last.* "Thank you." She walked up to where he stood and stared out over the water with him. The speedboat was a small dot on the horizon, but it seemed it was easier to look at the receding machine than each other.

"Yeah, well..." He cleared his throat and shrugged.

"I don't sleep around, either. Don't get me wrong, I've done my share of experimentation, but that was during my wild years."

"Wild years?"

She laughed and shook her head. "I've done more shit than a person my age has the right to do. Did you know at nine I was kicked out of school for organizing and staging a coup of the administration?"

He turned to look down at her. "What could be so drastically wrong with a school that you'd try to overthrow the administration?"

"Looking back, honestly, not much at all. At the time, though, my nine-year-old brain thought staging a revolt was the right thing to do. Needless to say, I was grounded for life. Homeschooling sucks. Just saying."

"Sounds safer for the community as a whole, though." He nudged her shoulder and she laughed.

"Or so my parents thought."

"Are you ever going to tell me who you are?"

"When I can, I will."

"So, something is stopping you from telling me?"

"*Someone* actually, but it is all going to be a moot point if I'm not allowed to do my job. This bullshit they've had us doing... I'm over it."

"Me, too." Smoke leaned over and picked up a set of air tanks. "I'll stow the equipment. If you still feel you need to make that call, the bridge is yours."

She picked up the belts and followed him to the storage lockers. "I'll put the call on hold for now. See where things go."

Smoke nodded as he bent down to put the tanks on the rack built into the storage locker. "Let's do that. See where things go." He looked up at her. "Where *everything* goes. No pressure on any aspect."

"I can deal with that." She headed back and picked up the other set of tanks and took them over to him so he could stow them. "Anything new from Guardian?"

The muscles in his arms strained as he took the tanks from her and maneuvered them into the rack. "They want pictures of people in the residence. We'll need to get the camera equipment and one hell of a big lens into our dive case. I'll move us in closer to the shoreline and we'll head out just after dusk. That will cover us when we come up at that outcropping." He pointed toward the shoreline. "We'll climb to the top and should have a good vantage point. The back of the house is nothing but glass, so we'll be able to get some good photos."

She sighed, "Photos. That makes me ask myself why I busted my ass in training at the Rose."

"Let's get up to the bridge and find out if there really was a missing fishing boat and get ready for the evening."

She glanced back to where the speed boat had disappeared. A niggle of worry raced across her skin. In the months she and Smoke had been floating in these waters, they'd never been approached by another boat. The occurrence was out of the norm, and one thing she'd learned early and fast was things outside the norm were to be examined and questioned. She turned and followed her partner to the bridge.

CHAPTER 4

Smoke glanced at the screen that monitored the sensors. *Fuck.* There was a new, three-lined readout. He'd be able to decipher them, but he didn't want Charley to see him as he was. Yet. He headed toward the secure comms. "Charley, what's the new information on the sensor readout?"

She headed over to the monitor. "Wow, this is… The sensors are indicating disturbances on sectors fifteen through eighteen. A ninety-second lull and then the same disturbance over and over again. Same sectors, although the timing is different with each sweep. It started… about ten minutes ago. Are they malfunctioning?"

"They shouldn't be." He put down the handpiece to the comms set and moved over to the console. "No, look, the indicator lights show they are functional."

Charley put down the readout and asked, "Do you want me to take a dive and check out the hull?"

"Wait, go back in the history and check at sunset yesterday. We had the sensors deployed, what was the disturbance when the sub or whatever it was went under us?"

She used the cursor arrows to move the screen. "Yeah, here…" She pointed to the lines. "So, what do we do with that?"

Smoke stared at the jumble of letters and then looked at her. "What do you make of it?" He'd become adept at redirecting questions to learn what was written.

"Well, the patterns have a similar sweep of the sensors, but that was one massive push causing these alarms. The indications today seem to indicate something swimming in and out of the sensors over and over again."

"And what does that?"

"Porpoise?"

"Or sharks, and yes, it could have been a person, but if you were rigging a boat this size to blow, would you take the time to swim in and out of the sensors to make sure you looked like a fish?"

"A porpoise isn't a fish, and I didn't see or hear any air blows this morning. I'm not liking the timing, either. It coincides too neatly to that weird 'Ahoy' dude showing up."

"Fish in the general term of living in the ocean, and I agree, the timing is suspect. Call CCS. We need someone to see if there is actually a missing boat. I'll take a look under her and see what is going on."

"Take the mask with the hardwired comms, I want to know what you see." Charley headed over to the receiver that he'd put down and looked back at him. "Well?"

"Has anyone ever told you that you are bossy?"

She snorted and turned her back on him. "All the time. Don't make me fuss at you for not following orders." She turned her head and gave him a once over. "Or maybe I'll take you over my knee and spank you."

Holy hell. *That would be a hard no.* He cleared his throat and started, "Ahh..."

She laughed and waved him off. "Not my kink, remember? Go, go, go." She made little shooing movements with her hand, and damned if he didn't find himself following her direction.

He headed to the back of the ship and grabbed a snorkel, face mask, and fins. No matter what his little dictator upstairs wanted, he wasn't going to bust out the specialty equipment unless he suspected something wrong. He sat on the locker and put on his fins and then flopped to the side of the boat where he scooped up water in his face-mask, making sure to wet the entire mask. If he didn't, the mask would fog and the rubber wouldn't seal as well. He put on the mask, sucked a couple large breaths of air before he put the snorkel in his mouth, and walked off the diving platform into the warm, azure blue waters.

It took several seconds for the bubbles to clear. When they did, he started his inspection. Diving down and returning up to get more air, he worked his way around the ship. The sensors swayed in the current of the water, but the system accounted for that movement. He dove down again and visually inspected the hull. There was nothing on this side. He resurfaced and made his way to the other side of the vessel. A half-hour later, he surfaced at the diving platform.

"You're an asshole sometimes, you know that?"

Charley yelled at him as soon as he popped his head above water.

He spit out his snorkel. "What?"

"Why didn't you take the comms?"

"Because I'm right here. If I needed you, I would have surfaced and whistled." He tossed his facemask and snorkel onto the deck and worked on freeing his feet from his fins. "What did Guardian say about the fishing vessel?"

"There was a report of a missing vessel this morning. Nothing else to substantiate the claim but it is logged with the Coast Guard."

"So, it could be true." He muscled himself out of the water and walked over to the storage lockers. He used one as a chair. "No disturbance, nothing attached that I could see."

"And you'd be able to see it, right?"

"I know where to look. Why are you asking? Are you afraid I missed something?" He glanced up at her. Her eyes were wide, and she shook her head.

"I know you wouldn't miss anything. I just don't like it. I got a bad feeling."

"About what specifically?"

"That guy this morning."

He slicked back his hair, wicking out the

seawater. “Yeah, his appearance doesn't settle well with me, either, but there *was* a report of a missing boat, and nobody has a clue what we're doing out here. Hell, we're six miles out. If we were watching any of the houses on that island, we'd be one hell of a lot closer.” He'd spent his recent silence and solitude while snorkeling around his ship running the scenarios through his mind. It gave him something to think about other than Charley as he searched for anything amiss on the hull. There was nothing. It had to be a coincidence.

“I don't like it.” She sat down beside him.

“Neither do I, but we can only do as much as we can.”

“Such as?”

“Get this surveillance done and maybe head back toward Key West. I have some friends there that I'd like you to meet.”

“In Key West? We've been there several times.” Realization dawned on her. “You didn't want me to meet your friends before because…?”

“Sage and I worked an operation with them in Cuba. I guess I didn't want to share that with anyone.” He extended his legs. The saltwater was drying on his skin, but he didn't care. He wanted to talk to Charley—really talk, not the polite visiting he'd kept it to until today.

"How is Sage doing?"

"He called me yesterday. He's not in a good place, but it was good that he called." He missed the hell out of his friend.

"Can I ask a question?" Charley tipped her head and a few strands of hair fell from her messy bun, sweeping the side of her arm.

"Another loaded question?" He laughed at her.

She shook her head. "Stop hiding behind your laughter, I'm being serious."

The fake smile slid off his face. "What?"

"It is rumored that you're bi, is that true?"

He lowered his gaze. Charley's legs dangled side to side with the roll of the craft. "I've had both men and women lovers, it's true."

"Do you love Sage? Are you in a relationship with him?"

He lifted his eyes to hers and answered honestly. "Yes, I love him, and yes, we are in a relationship, but not like you think."

"Then clarify it for me, would you?"

There was no anger in her words, no possessive bullshit or drama accompanying the question, and it was the one query he'd been dreading. Or rather, the series of inquiries that would follow. He was grateful her curiosity wasn't tainted with judgement or condemnation; rather, it seemed she was only interested in the truth. Another thing in the long list of things he liked about her. "Sage has a stuttering problem due to a traumatic brain injury when he was in the service. Before that, I gathered he didn't talk a lot; he was a loner, his upbringing kind of conditioned him to be that way. We were partnered on a smaller ship for a mission, and he couldn't avoid me, so I taught him to sign and he... well, he helped me with my limitation. I love him like a little brother. Nothing more and sure as hell, no less."

She was silent for a moment and they both stared off at the water. A million points of dancing light on the soft roll of the tide provided a blinding show of beauty. "What is your limitation?"

He turned at her question. He'd given her enough to deserve some blanks filled in, too. "Who are you?"

She sighed and dropped her head. "I can't tell you for a lot of reasons. Suffice to say I'm related to power brokers in this company."

He slapped his thigh. "I knew it. I damn well called it yesterday after I got off the phone with

Fury." He chuckled. "Well, I'm glad I know for sure, even though I don't think your connection to the management of Guardian is going to stop what's happening between us." He leaned back on his arms and stared at her. "Make sure this is what you want. That I'm what you want."

Charley mimicked his position and licked her lips. "Believe me, I *am* sure I want you, at least until my family pulls me from the field."

"Damn it, is that a possibility? How long until that could happen?" He'd have thought the Kings would be more receptive to someone in their family working in the field; after all, they all came up through the ranks. Well, except for Jewell. She'd always been a computer genius.

She shrugged. "I don't know. Depends on a lot of things. Maybe tomorrow, maybe next year. What is your limitation?"

"What?" He knew what she was asking, however. His response was to give himself a couple more seconds to brace himself for her reaction.

"You said that Sage helped you with your limitation. What limitation?"

He sat up and rubbed his suddenly damp palms against his board shorts. "I'm dyslexic."

She sat up, too, and stared at him. Finally, her brows creased. "That's it?"

"It's enough. I'm damn near illiterate."

Her eyes narrowed. "That's why you're not in Hollywood with your mom and brother."

He rolled his eyes. "Yeah."

"Wait, you sign to me when I'm on the dock and you don't want to yell."

"Signing isn't backward or upside down or tangled up with the jumble like those that are printed. I can guess at words because they have familiar patterns, but I one hundred percent can't deal with vowels. I mean, they don't make sense. Like I said, I can detect patterns in words, but not always. If you notice, I don't finger spell words. I generally skip that portion of my signing, but the context of what I'm saying is still carried to the person I'm signing to. That is how I understand you when you sign to me."

"Wow." She glanced off to her side for several seconds. "I never realized you didn't finger spell until you mentioned it."

He shrugged. "Guardian is aware of my problems. I don't need to know how to fingerspell or read to do the job I do for them."

"Wait, how do you learn about new developments in explosives?"

"Jewell or maybe the people in her section download the newest tech and convert it all into audio files. I get two or three files a month. I listen to them over and over and keep them for reference."

"So, signing helps?"

"It does. I don't know if it is a different component of my brain that processes the signs versus the letters, but I can and do understand signing. Printed words or finger spelling of words in ASL... God, I'm useless."

"Well, first and foremost, you are not useless. Second..." She punched his arm with a closed fist.

"Ouch! What the fuck, woman?"

"That is for being a stubborn asshole and not telling me so I could help you. What a pig-headed, macho, chest-thumping thing to do." She stood up and started pacing. "All this time... Wait, the reports and the maintenance logs?"

"I do them in my bedroom at night. The reports are easier because I use a dictation app. Maintenance and ship logs are harder. I spend a couple hours a night on them." He rubbed his shoulder. "Damn, you can land a punch, can't you?"

"Sage knew and you let him help, right?"

"We took care of each other."

"But you didn't trust me."

He stood and pushed back his half-dried hair. "I didn't want to *have* to trust you. I was comfortable with Sage and with our partnership. There was an ease between us, you know?"

She put her hands on her hips. "But there isn't that feeling between us?"

He shook his head slowly as he spoke, "Wasn't. And, woman, I don't think there is *anything* easy about you."

Charley slowly lifted a hand and extended her middle finger. "Fuck you, Smoke. You don't put this distance between us on me. I've been trying."

She was absolutely right. She had been trying; for months, he'd done nothing to enhance their partnership. "Fair enough. I'm sorry."

She dropped her hand and her eyes moved up and down his body. "Apology accepted. Is there anything else I need to know?"

"I think Joseph is going to hate me sooner rather than later."

"Why is that?"

"Why do you think?" He moved forward until he was right up in her personal space.

"I don't have any idea. Maybe you should explain it further." She lifted her arms around his neck.

"If I explain it further, we're going to get naked."

"I like naked."

He smiled and dipped down as if he was going to kiss her but stopped before his lips touched hers. "Thank God. Let's button her up and adjourn for some naked time."

Charley sighed and dropped her arms from around his neck. "Just when I think I'm going to get lucky."

He swatted her firm ass and ran up the stairs, laughing at her shriek of shock.

"Asshole, you did not just do that!"

He laughed harder and flew up to the next deck. He hadn't been this happy in a long, long time.

CHAPTER 5

The warm water sluiced off his shoulders and back as he scrubbed the saltwater residue off his skin. He'd left Charley on the bridge, asking her to look up the weather for tonight and tomorrow. As the water dulled the outside and centered him on the moment, he drew a deep breath and prayed the direction he and Charley were heading was the right one.

He placed the bar of soap back in the holder and reached for the shampoo. She was so damn young and… The bathroom door opened. He wiped the humidity off the glass shower door and blinked through the water drops on his eyelashes.

"Holy. Fuck."

Charley moved forward and opened the door,

beautifully naked, her tan lines outlining the swollen nipples of her breasts and the very apex of her sex. She stepped into the shower and brought all that naked skin against his. "You're even sexier than I imagined." Her hands traveled from his ribs to his pecs and then around his neck. "Fucking kiss me already, will you?"

His arms snaked around her now-slick skin and pulled her into him. He lowered his lips to hers and damn near died when their lips touched. High-octane, pure unadulterated sexual voltage in wattage he'd never experienced pounded through his veins. She had to have felt it, too. Her gasp as their tongues dueled and parried acted as an accelerant, and any thoughts of a slow first encounter burned up in the fuel of months worth of unanswered sexual tension.

She shoved him against the wall, and he countered, spinning her against the tile. He grabbed her leg, and she tightened her muscles, lifting her other leg up to his hip. He broke the kiss and grabbed her to stabilize them before they ended up on the floor of the shower. Fuck, that could happen anyway. A second of sanity flashed through his mind. "We need condoms." He bent down and bit her shoulder as his hips pushed forward. Fuck, he didn't want to stop.

She grabbed his face with both hands and forced him up to look at her. "I'm on birth control. If you stop now, I will do serious bodily harm to you."

He shook his head. "Not stopping." And fuck him, he wasn't. His cock was throbbing with the pulse of his blood through his veins. He grabbed her ass and pivoted, using her back to push open the shower door. Flipping the water off, he bounced them off walls and the door frame as they kissed. He felt the carpet under his feet as he staggered into the stateroom and headed in the general direction of the bed.

Charley bit his lip and then licked it before sucking it into her mouth. His shins hit the bed and he unceremoniously dropped to the mattress, pinning her under him. She didn't stop kissing him and, fucking hell, he wasn't going to make her stop. She wrapped her heels around his back, and he found her core. The tip of his cock pushed through to a blindingly tight, blissful heat. He tried to pull away from the kiss, to make sure she was on the same page one last time, but those strong arms held him tightly as her hips rocked up, encasing his shaft in ecstasy. His back arched, finally breaking their kiss. He stared down at her.

Her big brown eyes were half-open and there was a rose hue under her tan as she stared up at him. "I don't want slow and easy," she demanded as she arched under him.

He lifted onto his knees, pulling her up his thighs. "Damn good thing. Neither do I." He grabbed her hips and drove deep into her, adjusting slightly each thrust until she gasped and clenched the sheets hard enough to shred them. He fucked her with an intensity he rarely found. Her body under him was an erotic sight to behold as she responded to his moves. Charley was sex personified and she was his, at least for this moment in time. He grasped her tightly with one hand and slid the other to the top of her sex, teasing her clit with his thumb. He closed his eyes and fell into the sensations of their bodies. The excitement of the first kiss, the desperation fanned by months of denying his attraction to her and her innate sexuality pushed him toward his climax. God, he wanted her to come first, but he was so damn close.

Charley's muscles tightened, clenching around him, and he lost it. He let loose, his roar pulled from his lungs. He fell on top of her and thrust through the explosion, finally stilling in a boneless pool of satisfaction.

Charley's panting under him was the first thing that really registered. "Fuck." He attempted to put his arms under him and push off her.

She whispered, "Just… stay."

"I'm crushing you." He managed to lift his head to look at the woman below him.

"I'll live." She ran a finger down his back, and he shivered from the intensity of the small touch. "I'll give you credit, Gramps. You got game."

He dissolved into laughter as did she. He rolled off her onto his side and she turned, mimicking his position. They stared at each other. He took in her youth, her beauty, and her flush of satisfaction. He knew what she saw: his brother's face. But maybe this time the person he was with would look deeper. It hadn't happened often. Once, in fact, and that instance had ended in a spectacular fashion.

"Where did you just go?" Charley reached out and placed a hand on his chest, jolting him out of his memories.

"I'm right here."

"Your body is, your mind went somewhere dark, didn't it?"

He sighed and nodded. “How could you tell?”

“I've been watching you for months. I can see the humor you hide behind and I can see when you're hurting, which is a hell of a lot more than you let on.” She snuggled closer to him and he dropped his chin on top of her head. “It must have been hell for you growing up.”

Hell? No, hell would have been an improvement. “It wasn't easy.”

“You never lived with your mom?”

“Or my dad. I was sent away.”

She tightened and asked, “Away? Where to?”

He sighed. “A group home for the mentally diminished.”

She arched back so she could look up at him. The anger in her eyes was not what he expected.

“I want to visit your family. After dark. With a gun.”

He chuckled and leaned forward to kiss her. “Thank you, but they are not worth the jail time.”

She narrowed her eyes at him. “Who said I'd get caught? I'm working with a Shadow. Oh! I know, I can practice that land-based explosive training we've been going over.”

He pushed her long hair back off her face. “I've come to terms with the fact that my family was horrid. I left as soon as I could, and I've never contacted them. Guardian is my family now."

"The offer stands. I'll hook them up in a heartbeat." Charley snuggled closer to him again as she spoke.

He wrapped her in his arms and closed his eyes. "Noted."

"How did you get involved with Guardian?"

"I broke into a construction site and stole some blasting caps, det cord, and a half-box of TNT." He'd been hired to pick up trash on a demolition site and had loitered, watching the men who used the explosives to break up huge boulders that littered the build site. They even showed him what they were doing when they saw he was interested.

She chuckled. "What did you blow up?"

"The group home. I went back. I pulled the fire alarm and made sure everyone was out before I blew it up."

"Why?"

He closed his eyes and recalled every abuse the caretakers had dispensed against the residents of the home. The physical and mental assaults, locking residents in closets, tying them to chairs, not feeding them if they didn't follow instructions that most couldn't understand. The bruises he and the other residents carried when the attendants wanted punching bags. He'd seen three residents die in that home. He cleared his throat. "I'm sure you can imagine. Unsupervised and unqualified people in charge of special needs residents. It wasn't..."

She was quiet for a while before she spoke again. "You didn't just blow up the home, did you?"

"No. I watched three people die in that place. They were murdered as sure as if those people had put a gun to their head. I knew the residents couldn't testify and no one would believe me. I was just a simpleton after all. I found them, I stalked them, and I made them pay."

"That's when Demos found you."

He opened his eyes and moved away from her. "How do you know Demos?"

She blinked and opened her mouth to speak but snapped it shut again. He stared at her, watching her mind work behind those big eyes. She shrugged, almost to herself, and then answered. "Through my family connections. There isn't much about Guardian I don't know or haven't pieced together."

He nodded. That made sense. Being a King would put you in the know about everything, and she'd been through the Rose, so she knew about pairing shadows with regular operatives like her. "Yeah, that's when he found me. He took me in and gave me a purpose and a place to excel. He once told me that my intelligence and desire to learn far exceeded my limitation, making it a moot point. He said if I used my dyslexia as a crutch, he'd be disappointed in me. I sure as fuck didn't want to disappoint him. He was and still is who I consider my father."

"Demos is a good man, his wife wouldn't have it any other way," she agreed and yawned. "We need sleep if we are going for a swim later."

He made a sound of agreement and closed his eyes, enjoying the contact and the small connection they shared, both knowing and admiring a person who was important in his life. Demos was a damn good man.

CHAPTER 6

Charley emerged from the water about thirty seconds after Smoke. He was a stronger swimmer and had a grace in the water she couldn't ever hope to achieve. His minimal movement, maximum power, and complete efficiency were breathtaking to watch, but the only thing she saw tonight in the darkness of the water was his leg which had a glow stick attached to it. The muted light would be impossible to see from above, but she could follow it in the dark water. She removed her regulator and deflated the buoyancy compensator before removing her fins and following Smoke up onto the rocky shoreline. She glanced at her dive computer attached to her wrist while he removed the glow stick from his wetsuit. Thirty-seven minutes underwater and over half her oxygen tank left for the return trip. They secured the equipment and pulled on water shoes so they could climb up the rocky embankment.

Smoke handed her the case when they crested the top of the hill across the small bay from the house they were assigned. "Damn, that's a freaking mansion," Smoke muttered as she handed him the camera.

She gave a second look at the small house on the cliff across from them. The floor-to-ceiling glass on the back of the house had to be a bitch to protect during hurricanes. There were a few lights on in the home. Hopefully, the occupants would be somewhere taking in the view so they could get some photos to send to Guardian. Then she'd contact Joseph and find out *who* was keeping her in training wheels. She was supposed to be proving herself here, not bobbing around the water and wasting what precious time she had. Everyone was afraid of Fury. Not her. Nope. Although he was deadly, he was also a devoted family man. Family gatherings were a great way to scope out how far she could push without getting shoved back into a corner. That corner sucked and she never wanted to go back. Yeah, there would be zero issues going toe to toe with the assassin to find out why she was being hogtied.

"Anything?" she asked as Smoke moved the camera.

"No. No one." He handed her the camera and twisted to sit with his back against the rock while she tried to find the people they were supposed to track. She moved the camera to the left and right.

"There are shutters up on the house to the right. I say we move closer." She dropped the camera and looked at her partner.

"We'd need to snorkel over." Smoke turned and stared at the small bay they'd have to swim across. "Maybe two thousand meters, but the water looks calm."

"Sounds lovely." She handed Smoke the camera and opened the case again to repack the equipment. "No one at home?"

"Not that I can see. Guardian said the signal was still coming from the location." They worked themselves back down the embankment and suited up again. Comms to Guardian weren't in the plans tonight. As good as the comm equipment was, it wasn't waterproof. She made sure her snorkel was attached to the left side of her mask and glanced over at Smoke. He gave her a thumbs-up which she returned. They slipped under the warm water and made their way across the small, sheltered bay. Tracking him was much easier on top of the water. The process to remove the equipment and scale the rock wall was made easier by a set of wooden steps on the far side of the adjacent property. They jogged up and darted into the darkest part of the yard. She opened the case and Smoke stared through the lens. "I need to get closer."

They edged forward, changing angles so they were almost directly in front of the other house, shielded by a clump of flowering lantana bushes. She settled next to Smoke and stared at the house. "It's empty."

He nodded, taking pictures in a systematic way until he stopped, dropped the camera, and then immediately jerked it up again. "Fuck, get going. Go! Run to the equipment." He pushed her and they scrambled from behind the bush.

"What's going on?" She hissed the question as they sprinted across the yard, heading for the open gate and the stairs to the water.

"It's a trap."

His words pushed her down the stairs faster than anything else could. They threw on the tanks and masks and plunged into the water, camera forgotten along with the dive fins. She followed Smoke, keeping close so she could feel his wake to guide her in the darkness of the night. He slowed and tugged her arm and she surfaced with him.

Smoke glanced around and oriented himself. They were diving blind. She pulled her oxygen regulator out of her mouth and treaded water with him. "What did you mean a trap?"

"Guardian said the guy collected pocket watches, that's what they were tracking, right? An expensive motherfucking watch, right?"

She treaded water and listened, but he said nothing further as he looked around them. "Yes, so?"

"And there was a pocket watch dismantled on a table right by the window."

"How is that a trap?"

"It was sitting by a block of C4, cell phone trigger."

"Damn it! Why? How did they know? We made no moves toward them; they couldn't know it was us assigned to them."

"I think the trap is for whoever shows up at the

house." He spun around and nodded. "We don't have a glow stick. I want you beside me the entire time we're below the surface. If you lose contact with me and can't find me, surface and I'll do the same, we'll reconnect and go again."

"Got it." She put the register in her mouth just as a golden streak arched through the air. "Oh shit." Her mumbled comment spun Smoke just as the rocket exploded midship of his yacht. She heard his scream of anger as a second rocket launched from the island and hit his ship again.

"Come on! We have to get to the shore." She pulled on his arm, physically moving him, but his attention riveted on his home that was consumed in yet another explosion. "Damn it, Smoke! *Move!*"

He let off with a long string of expletives, some she'd never heard and doubted were actual words. "That way." He pointed, shoved his register in his mouth, and waited for her to nod her understanding. They took off at a pace that would have winded an Olympic sprinter. She kept up, but it was damn hard to maintain the pace he held. Confusion was the only thing that she felt. *How did they know?*

They crawled up on a small cove and stowed

the gear behind some rocks and scrub brushes. When a person is angry, really life-altering angry, they don't want to talk. She knew it and she gave Smoke a wide berth, following his lead as he started to climb the rock outcropping leading to the top of the island. They topped the rocks and lay on the edge, assessing their location. A road wound close to the ledge where they laid. From where they were, they could see lights. A small town probably. As far as she was concerned, there was no need for her to move again in the next twenty-four hours or so. That wish yesterday for a damn good workout... Well, fate had granted it to her in triplicate.

Smoke rolled onto his back. "The safes held. There weren't any secondary explosions." His stash of explosives was neatly stacked in two massive safes the previous owner had used for his ill-gotten gains.

"You'll have to salvage the safes, won't you?"

"Everything is wrapped individually in a waterproof container. Living on a ship, you take precautions."

She hummed her agreement but kept a watch, not wanting to be highlighted by the headlights of some random vehicle.

He cussed low under his breath. "How did they know we weren't on the ship?"

She shook her head and quietly added, "Maybe they actually thought we *were* on board. The question I'm baffled by is *why* would they blow up the ship?"

"To keep us from getting off the island or from following them." Smoke closed his eyes. "Think, damn it." He scrubbed his face with his hand. "We need to get to a phone."

She nodded. "Lights in that direction or we can go back to the house next to the rigged one and break in."

He lifted and looked in the direction of the lights and then back toward the abandoned trap. "They wouldn't expect us to go back."

"I don't want to get blown up, but I agree. If someone is looking for us, it won't be there, it will be expected that we head toward civilization."

"We stay as far away from that house as possible. Get in, make a call, and get out." Smoke glanced back at the water. "Quickest way."

Charley nodded. "We can assume cameras, surveillance of the approach from the water and from the street."

"If we stay due west of the closed-up house

and somehow manage to get in from that direction we shouldn't be sighted. If we move to the front or the rear of the house, we'll be visible again."

"I'll fucking bore a hole in it with my teeth if I have to," Charley said as they stood and made their way to the edge of the road. Her water shoes squished under her feet but thank goodness they'd dove into the water without changing them out for flippers. The coral alongside the road would have shredded their feet within a mile if they were forced to walk barefoot.

They worked their way back toward the three houses on the cliffside, ducking out of sight when a stray vehicle's headlights announced its meandering arrival. They moved away from the road about a mile from the homes, putting the house with the hurricane shutters directly between them and the house with the suspected surveillance system and waiting block of C4.

"Shit." She looked up at the windows that were shuttered. Smoke leaned in toward her. "See that power meter?"

"Yeah?" She saw it, but what the hell good would it do her?

"I'm going to lift you up; you get your feet on

top of it and you can slide the metal panel of the window beside it."

"How do I open it?" She was gauging the distance from where she'd be standing to the window.

"There are tracks at the top and bottom, see them?" She nodded. "Just use the toe of your shoe and push it toward the front of the house. If we need to break the glass, the sound should be dampened by the shutters."

She swiveled her attention to him. "And what about alarms?"

"We are a long way from a police station. By the time they'd get halfway here, Guardian could do its magic and turn off the response. Maybe." Smoke shrugged. "It's our only play unless you see another."

She stared at the side of the house. "No, I don't see any other option."

"Then let's go."

Charley followed him to the side of the house and put her foot in his cupped hand. With his power under her, she vaulted up and grabbed the iron tube above the meter to pull herself up on top of the device. The force of his lift damn near catapulted her past the top of the meter. She held herself against the house and found balance on her tiptoes of one foot. Unfortunately, it was the wrong foot. She drew a deep breath and carefully felt around with the toe of her other swim shoe until she found a tiny spot to balance. Thank God her mother made her take ballet lessons. She lifted her foot in perfect point and leaned forward, inching the heavy metal. Her sweaty hands slipped against the galvanized pipe she was holding. Cranking her grip as tight as she could, she leaned to the side.

"I'm here. I'll catch you if you fall." Smoke's reassurance wasn't needed, but it was appreciated. She pointed her toe and pushed.

The metal slid away, and she went down. Her foot caught on the window ledge and she bridged the span of distance in a straddle split. "Oh, fuck."

"Well, that's one hell of a talent I wasn't aware of."

She rolled her eyes. "Asshole, I'm stuck." She hissed the words because while she was limber, she hadn't stretched for this straddle and it freaking hurt like a mother.

"Fall straight back. I'll catch you."

She hissed, "I'll fall headfirst!"

"Let go, there's a car coming."

Shit! She clenched her eyes shut and pushed off the side of the house, falling backward.

The collision of their bodies was controlled, but they both landed on the ground. She groaned and rolled off the top of her partner. "I thought you were going to catch me. Did the car see us?"

Smoke sat up and rolled his neck and shoulders. "There wasn't a car. I said that to get you to drop."

Charley whipped around and punched him on the shoulder.

"Hey! What the fuck was that for?" He rubbed his arm.

"Oh, I don't know. Let's start with lying to your partner and end up with, oh... Lying to your partner! Asshole." She stood up and offered him a hand.

He looked at her and shook his head. "Uh-uh, I can see it. You're planning on hitting me again."

"Damn straight, I am. Now, get up and lift me up to the window so we can get in and call Guardian. They probably think we're dead."

Smoke stood and stretched. "Anyone ever tell you that you are not light?"

She braced her hands on her hips. "You know,

with lovely lines like that you might not get any sex again."

She saw him smile, the asshole. "You know you want me as much as I want you. Stop making empty threats." He squatted down. "Get on my shoulders and I'll lift you up."

Arguing didn't seem to be the best course of action because, in fact, she *did* want him again—in a myriad of positions. So, she scrambled up his back and up to his shoulders. With him standing, she could pull herself up to the window ledge. She heaved herself up, struggling to stand on his shoulders. "Stop moving," she hissed at him.

"Then stop stepping on my head." His hands grabbed her ankle and repositioned it as she leaned against the window ledge. "There, open the fucking window, please."

She glared down at him, but the dark and the fact that he wasn't looking up made the gesture moot. She palmed her dive knife and jimmied the lock of the double-hung window. She re-sheathed her knife and placed her palms against the glass, sliding it up. Charley grabbed the inside of the window ledge and pulled herself up and into the… dining room. She opened the window farther and slid the metal shutter even more so Smoke's shoulders could get through the opening.

"Let me find something to use as a rope."

"No need."

She watched him back up and then run toward the house. He planted a foot on the side of the structure and launched toward the window, grabbing the window ledge with one hand. His second hand landed inside the window, and he pulled himself through the opening, sliding to the floor. She slid the shutter back, enclosing them in darkness.

Slumping against the wall, she drew a deep breath. "You realize this is going to suck massively if they don't have a landline phone."

Smoke's head whipped up. "Woman, stop with the negative vibes."

Charley blinked and dropped her head to look at him. "Vibes? Isn't that a 1960s saying? I mean, I know you're old, but no way you're *that* old."

"Vibes is not a 60's saying." He stood and cracked his back. "God, that felt good."

She laughed and followed him out the door. "Vibes *is* an ancient word. If I were a landline, I'd be in the main bedroom or the kitchen."

"All right. I'll take the kitchen; the bedroom would be..."

"That way." They said the words together. She pointed to the left and he pointed to the right. He made a groaning noise in the back of his throat and turned right, she turned left. The stairs around the corner put a smile on her face. She jogged up them using the banister as a guide. The first room was a small bedroom, ditto for the second door. The third was a bathroom, the main was at the end of the hall. And there, beside the four-poster bed, was an old-fashioned, hard-wired phone. She lifted it off the receiver and heard Smoke talking to the operator. "Be advised, the line has been compromised." The operator's level voice never changed.

"Thorn Operative Twenty-Two online," she acknowledged her presence.

"Stand by."

"I see you found the kitchen."

"And you found the bedroom," Smoke chuckled.

She stared at the closets. "We're going to need clothes."

"And a shower."

"What the fuck happened?" Fury's voice ripped across the line.

"We went for a swim to do the surveillance as requested. The house is a trap. The pocket watch is completely disassembled and sitting on a package of C4 with a cell phone trigger. We got the hell away from the house, and that's when some motherfucker blew my boat out of the water."

"How did they get explosives on your boat without setting off your sensors?" Fury demanded.

"They fired three rockets at it," Charley finished.

"M72 is my bet," Smoke added.

"Where are you now?"

"At the house next door to your bogey," Smoke answered for them.

There was silence for a while. "I'll make sure you're secure. Stand by for a call." The phone went dead, and Charley put the receiver down. She made her way to the closet and was damn near blinded by the light that turned on when she opened the door. *Oh, definitely promising*. She heard Smoke enter the bedroom. "That one should have clothes for you." She pointed across the room and he promptly made a detour.

There were racks and racks of dresses, but no

shorts or jeans. Charley muttered, "Someone must have a dress fetish."

"What do you think?" She spun around to look at what he was holding and burst into laughter as Smoke danced a lime green nylon leisure suit on the hanger.

"No. Just no."

"Damn, I thought I had a winner. I think I could rock that color."

"Nah, your color palette leans more toward warmer tones."

His brow creased and he cocked his head. "Am I supposed to know what that means?"

She sniggered, "No, but your self-obsessed doppelganger would."

Smoke snorted and shoved the suit back on the rod and fanned through the rest of the clothes while she continued her hunt. Finally settling on a pale-yellow sundress that she could cinch at the waist and a pair of sandals that were only about one size too big, she glanced back at Smoke. He'd laid out a large tropical print shirt and a pair of khaki pants on the bed.

Motioning to the slacks, she shook her head. "They're not going to fit." It was obvious the inseam was at least ten inches too short.

"All I need is a pair of scissors and presto, they're shorts. I'll have to cut the belt down and punch a hole or ten, but it will keep them up. Going to have to wear my swim shoes, though. The man has really small feet."

"His wife makes up for it." She held up the sandals and the dress. "But I can work with these." At least until they got money and visited a store that sold more age-appropriate clothing.

The phone rang and Smoke picked up the receiver. She lifted to her tiptoes and pulled on his arm so she could hear, too.

"Authenticate Powder," Fury's voice cracked over the connection.

"Keg," Smoke replied and nodded to the bed where they both sat down so she could hear easier.

"CCS online," Jewell's voice came through the connection.

"Annex online," Anubis added.

"Alpha," Jacob chimed in.

"Archangel. Bring me up to speed." Jason's gravelly voice was impossible to miss.

"Smoke, give it to them from the horse's mouth," Fury demanded. She listened as Smoke detailed the events of the last three hours.

"Smoke is probably right. I trust his judgement.

The bogey hasn't moved since yesterday morning. I've tried to hack into the security system in the house using the telephone company's lines, local cable, and satellite providers, but there doesn't seem to be a hackable connection to get a look at the security footage. We're still trying, but my gut tells me the system is either encrypted up the wazoo or there isn't a connection available. I'm betting on the second, probably a standalone closed-loop security surveillance system. It's what I'd do if I wanted to keep an eye on my property."

Jacob commented, "Yeah, but how would you monitor it?"

"With notifications to my cell," Jewell responded immediately.

"So, the system is transmitting," Charley heard Jewell's husband say in the background.

"Yeah, but on which carrier, to what number? I mean, I know the population on Grand Cayman isn't huge, but that's a lot of phones to scrub through."

She pulled the phone down closer to her and asked, "Jewell, could you narrow the search to out-of-country numbers or maybe even just one number? There is a cell attached to the trigger. What if the guy is using his cell or one of his traveling companion's as a triggering device? Could you isolate the number that—"

Jewell squealed. "Ping the local towers, narrow down devices in the area, and cross-match with other phones from similar locality to map movements. Charley, you are so damn smart. Stand by."

She put her hand over the receiver and whispered to Smoke, "That wasn't what I was suggesting, but it sure made me look a lot smarter than I am."

He winked at her. The action was sexy, flirtatious, and downright inviting. It was an effort to tune into what the others were saying, but she managed. Just.

"We'll need to extract Smoke and Charley." Jason's voice snapped her eyes to Smoke's.

"From the house they are located at, I agree. From the mission, I do not," Fury countered.

There was an audible sigh. "She could have been aboard that ship tonight when it was attacked."

"Jason, could I speak to you? Alone." Fury's grated request hissed across the connection.

"Oh, hell no. This is my life. If you two are deciding my future, I'm in on it." Charley ripped the phone out of Smoke's hand. "I'm on a landline.

Smoke is leaving." She stared at him and he lifted his eyebrow. She shook her head and lifted her eyes to the door. He didn't like it, she could tell, but he moved across the room and closed the door silently behind him. "My end is secure." She said to the dead space of the call.

"Do you want me to sanitize the line?" Jewell asked.

"Just the three of us Jewell, blank us out for three minutes. No longer."

"Rog-O." Jewell's tapping in the background stopped. "You'll be clear in three, two, one."

"I'm a trained operative. What the fuck is going on? You had requirements for me to go through the program. I surpassed every damn one of them. Don't force me out before I have to leave." She ground the words out.

"And if you die? What do I tell your mom and dad?"

"What do you tell every other parent? The truth, that I died serving my country."

"It's not the same and you know it. Your parents are—"

"My concern. How many other operatives do you throttle to keep them safe?" There was silence on the other end of the line. "Joey, you know I'm qualified."

"Little girl, I will tan your hide for that, only my wife calls me Joey."

"I'm *sooo* scared, you'd never touch me. Now, if we could get back to business, you know I'm damn good. I earned my stripes. Take the handcuffs off me, Jace. *Please*."

"This operation could expose things you don't want revealed. Things that can never be put back into a nice, neat box. Besides, the primary in this case could have a team of assassins working for him," Jason warned.

"Like *we* don't? Smoke, for one, and because of his training he is more than capable of backing me up if I need it. Listen, if exposure is the cost, I'll pay it, but I'll leave knowing what I'm capable of doing. Smoke deserves a real partner, one that isn't shoved into a corner and blocked from working."

"Smoke is our lynchpin between the original assassins and the newer classes. He's just as critical as you are, and I am well aware of what he deserves. But when the shit hits the fan, you know what will happen," Jason reminded her.

"I do and I'm at peace with it." She'd had a fairly long reprieve from the storm looming on her horizon, but she'd face it when it came and remember every minute of every day she'd lived her life on her terms.

"Call Smoke back in. We have twenty seconds until everyone else comes back on the line. And Charley?"

She paused. "Yes?"

"Don't presume to question my authority again. I can and will take you off any mission I don't deem suitable for your skills." Jason's rebuke stung, but in all fairness, she deserved it.

"I copy all." She cupped her hand over the mouthpiece and called for Smoke. He walked back in almost immediately, so he was just outside the door either waiting or listening. Whatever, she would never say anything that would compromise her identity, even on secure comms.

"Annex on."

"Alpha on."

"CCS back, and I have three other cell phones with the same country code as the one in the house next to you."

"How did you narrow it down?"

"Easy, it's the only cell operational in three miles in any direction," Jewell responded. "The other three phones traveled west and are located in the general area of Georgetown."

"Anubis, where is the other asset?"

"Georgetown." The answer came back quickly. Charley glanced at Smoke, who shrugged, obviously not knowing there was another asset in the area, either.

"Jewell, after we clear here, send those coordinates to Anubis, who will contact his asset and have him monitor, and if possible, photograph the three individuals."

Anubis cleared his throat. "Sir, Reaper is not... subtle. He isn't the one you want for this mission. I can bring in someone else."

There was a long pause. "No. Charley, you and Smoke proceed to Georgetown. Jacob, get them identification, money, and whatever else two homeless people are going to need."

"Weapons, comms, and clothing to start," Jacob interjected.

"Yes, please. Grampa Gus' clothes are going to call attention to us," Smoke added with a chuckle. "But seriously, we have nothing. We lost everything when the ship went down." There was a physical sense of loss communicated through his words. Losing his home fucking sucked and he wasn't hiding it.

"I'm sorry about that, Smoke. It was always a risk," Jason sighed.

"I know. One I was happy to take. I just need you to find me another drug kingpin who has a better yacht. I'll commandeer it and start over."

"Sounds like a plan. I'll get right on that," Fury chuckled.

"Here is the down and dirty. The individual that purchased that pocket watch is an American by the name of Darryl Clayborne and we suspect he has built a shadow organization based on a limited amount of information he received when he was being considered for recruitment into our organization. He currently works for the North Korean government but has altered his appearance. Additionally, we believe he is using his little cabal of killers to moonlight. The name they collectively assassinate people under is Akuma." Jason pushed through the briefing in a rapid clip. "Our mission is to get a positive identification of Clayborne and take him out but only after we confirm the ID."

Her jaw dropped and she asked, "How?" The same question echoed from Smoke.

"I'm sure the two of you will figure something out." Jason stated. "Unless you don't think you can accomplish this mission."

"We've got it." Smoke's response was terse, but she'd have gone a bit farther and added 'asshole' at the end of it, so it was better he spoke for them.

Jason continued, "Perfect. You two get to Georgetown. Anubis, have Reaper observe but not engage. Hopefully, he can keep from crashing through Georgetown himself until Smoke and Charley arrive in the morning."

"I'll make sure of it, sir," Anubis acknowledged.

"Jacob, I want a team in the Caribbean."

"Roger that, what island and can I have a pilot and small aircraft? It would enable island hopping for all assets or a movement to CONUS if necessary." He rattled off the request to Jason.

"Affirmative. Fury, I'll need someone to cover the territory Smoke and Charley were assigned. They are locked on this mission. Open bore, no restrictions. Archangel out."

"You got your wish, little girl. Make the best of it. Fury out."

"Anubis out."

"I'll send those items down immediately, but you'll need to lay low for twenty-four to forty-eight hours. Coordinate the pickup through Reaper after he makes contact. Alpha out."

"So, there are two registered vehicles to that address. Mr. and Mrs. Kenworth are British citizens and... yep, they have a return trip ticket for six weeks from now. Probably one vehicle left in the garage if they took one to the airport. One of my people will call you tonight if the cells move, but only after they inform Reaper, of course. Contact this office when you move toward Georgetown and we'll make the proper notifications. Thanks for the nudge, Charley, sometimes I can't see the trees for the forest."

"I won't tell anyone I was going to suggest you try to backtrack that phone's call history."

"You realize any electronic surge to that device, even in the boot-up system, could activate the phone's screen and blow the entire house to smithereens, right?"

"Yeah, I do. Smoke taught me that. Hence the part where I *wasn't* going to tell you what I was going to suggest."

Jewell laughed. "You guys good for the night or do I need to make some magic happen and get you rooms in Georgetown?"

"We'll stay here. It's vacant and no one should

come looking for us, there was no alarm panel by the fuse box, no sensors on the windows or inside the doors that I could see," Smoke spoke for the first time in a while.

"I'll have one of ours monitor any traffic from the local police departments, but we haven't keyed in on anything yet, so you're more than likely correct. Sleep with one eye open anyway," Bengal interjected.

"I always do. Whatever it takes, my friend."

"As long as it takes. CCS out."

CHAPTER 7

Smoke hung up the phone and stared at the shower where he should be heading, but he couldn't move without telling her he'd heard every word she'd said to Jason and Joseph.

"How much did you hear?" Charley asked as she walked into the bathroom and turned on the shower.

"Enough to wonder what the hell you have on them to get away talking to them that way."

A low chuckle came from the bathroom along with the sounds of her wetsuit zipper being opened. "Not a damn thing. I guess familiarity breeds the casualness."

He stood up and moved to the doorway in time to watch her wiggle out of the neoprene suit. All that golden-tan flesh exposed to his view was tempting, damned tempting. But there was a question he needed answered. “What will exposure cost you?”

She peeked over at him as she pulled the wetsuit off her leg. “Everything, but that's on me, not you.”

“Who are you afraid of?”

She chuckled and tugged the suit off her other leg. “Nobody.”

“Then who will find out if you're exposed? I need to know what's going on. We're partners.”

She snorted and turned her back to him. “That's what I've been saying for the last four months, remember?”

“Yeah, I was a dick, but I thought we'd moved past that.” He grabbed the string attached to the zipper on his back and tugged it down, opening the suit so he could work himself out of it.

Charley stepped into the shower and pulled the door shut. Raising her voice, she answered, “We have moved past your dickishness, but I'm not about to let you forget it.”

Smoke tugged at the neoprene. “That's fair. I guess.”

“To answer your question though, you don't

need to worry about who will find out or what will happen if they do. It has nothing to do with this mission or what we are being instructed to do. I had to have that 'come to Jesus' meeting with those two macho mentalities. Otherwise, they'd wrap me in cotton batting and shove me in a corner for the rest of my natural life."

He kicked out of his suit and stood up, popping his back as he did. "Which is basically what they did when they put you on my ship with me."

"Yep." She moved over as he stepped into the shower. "Which isn't fair to you or me. The lessons you've taught me about explosives have been exemplary, my knowledge base has expanded exponentially, and I'm now a master diver, but seriously, this isn't what I was trained for nor is Guardian using your talents."

"So, are you comfortable with me having your back?" He turned her around in the shower as he asked and leaned forward, placing his wet skin against hers.

Her hands gripped his hips and she pulled herself closer. She turned her head and quietly whispered. "Why don't you ease my mind and show me how you can take care of my six?" A small swivel of her hips against his groin hardened his already-interested cock.

He thrust his cock up between the cheeks of her ass and she purred. Fucking purred like a cat. He lowered his lips to her ear. "Teasing or promising?"

She brought a hand up and palmed his neck. "Promising. Anything you want you can take."

His hand traveled from her hip to her stomach and lower, splitting the folds of her sex and finding her clit. Her body lurched forward in an uncontrolled response to his pressure against that sensitive nub. "Should I make you come like this?"

Her head dropped back onto his shoulder. "No."

"But you promised me anything I wanted. I want to watch you come from just my fingers."

She moaned and closed her eyes. He trailed kisses down her exposed neck and his hand found a rhythm and a pressure that made her body vibrate under his touch. His free hand found her nipples. He rolled them gently, first one then the other as he continued to stimulate her and kiss her exposed shoulder and neck. Her breathing changed, and she strained against him, looking for more friction or perhaps a faster tempo, but he hadn't lied. He wanted to see her come from just this. No more, no less.

Her hands gripped his forearms and her nails dug into his skin. His hips thrust against her slippery body. The hot water fogged the glass enclosure, bringing the world to a pinpoint focus. It was Charley. She was his entire world at this moment. The need for her hadn't diminished after the first time. Charley was delicious, a feast to be savored, sipped, and luxuriated in. His greed yesterday had only quenched the tiniest portion of the thirst he'd ignored. Months of his stupid denial and deflection had left him famished. *What a fool.*

Her body shook under his touch, and a pleading keen sounded as her hips drove forward into his hand and back into his thrusting cock. He hadn't entered her; he didn't need any more stimulation. His own desire had reached a critical juncture, and he dropped his hand to hold her against him. A bit faster, a little harder with his hand stimulating her and the friction of her against his cock, urging his own release. He watched it happen. Her head dropped back, her mouth opened slightly, and her eyes clenched closed. The tightening and releasing rolled through her and she gasped, holding his forearms in a death grip, her nails drawing blood. The sting of her piercing his skin and the beauty of her climax was all he needed. He came as he thrust against the wet skin of her pert ass.

It was all he could do to keep them both upright. Their ragged breathing slowed as they recovered under the flood of hot water. She licked her lips and sighed. "Fuck, no one has ever…"

Smoke chuckled. "Young men don't have enough sense to enjoy every facet of knowing a woman."

She hummed her agreement and turned in his arms, wrapping hers around his neck, her beautiful eyes hooded with sated desire. "Boys have no idea how to please a woman."

"I'll take that as a compliment."

"Please do." She lifted on her toes and he tasted her lips for the first time since they left the ship.

He let the kiss linger until the water started to turn cold. They soaped up and got out of the shower. Charley wrapped a towel around herself and announced, "I'm hungry. I'm going to see what they have in the kitchen. Meet me there when you get done, okay?"

"Be there in a minute." He turned off the shower and grabbed a towel from the bar. So much had happened in such a short time. Perspective had a way of bitch-slapping a person when they least expected it. He remembered watching his home sink into the water; he realized the only thing that couldn't be replaced on that vessel was the woman he'd just held in his arms. Everything except Charley. She was, in fact, his partner—and now his lover. He wasn't the man she needed in her life. She had so many things to see, discover, and enjoy. Things he'd never be able to do with her because of who he was, or rather, who he was related to. His brother had become so famous that at times he felt a hindrance to Guardian more than an asset. It was why he banished himself to his ship. He didn't need the bright lights, parties, or social events. He was a loner by nature, but Charley... Well, he couldn't imagine her happy spending her life with someone like him.

He pulled on his borrowed boxers, clean and by all accounts ironed before they were put into the dresser. They fell immediately, the curve of his ass keeping them from falling all the way down. He tugged them up and held onto the waistband as he padded down to the kitchen.

Charley gave him a quick smile. "The pantry has a bounty, plus there is wine or liquor." She pointed with a can opener she had in her hand. "I have crackers here, potted meat, nuts, and look, caviar!"

"We should leave a note thanking them for their hospitality." He tugged his boxers up and headed toward the liquor cabinet. He'd have one and then call it. He wasn't lying when he told Bengal he'd sleep with one eye open. They were not where the fuckheads thought they'd be, and before long, it would be light. If he were the asshats that had fired on his ship, he'd examine every fucking swim out from the house next door to where his home used to be, then he'd start the hunt.

"Would you pour me a small one? I don't want to be impaired, but I sure as fuck am celebrating the fact that we are alive and temporarily out of danger," Charley called to him from the table where she was prepping their meal.

A smile crossed his face as he poured her the same amount that he'd poured himself. "We should leave before light."

"Yeah, and instead of driving straight into Georgetown, I thought maybe we'd go around the island and come in from the other direction. If they are waiting or looking for us, they will be concentrating their efforts on this side of the island."

Smoke shook his head. "While that makes sense, we'll have to drive by the front of that house. The camera and security system they were using will pick up the vehicle and us in it."

He handed her the cup, and she took it, staring at him with her eyes narrowed. "We can disguise ourselves as the owners. We're wearing their clothes. You can slouch down so you're barely up over the steering wheel. I'll grab a sweater and maybe push tissue or something into the arms. Maybe she has a wig, but if she doesn't, I can put my hair up and use baby powder on it to change the color."

He took a sip of his whiskey and shook his head. "You have an active imagination, don't you?"

She took a sip of her whiskey and hummed an affirmative sound. "Better than most, I expect, but I don't think looking at things from a slightly different perspective is wrong. Do you?"

"No, it's what makes each of us unique." He sat down after he pulled out her chair for her and seated her.

"That was nice."

He glanced at her. The sex? The sex was better than nice. Wasn't it? "What?"

"Pulling out my chair for me. A gentlemanly thing to do. Where did you learn that? I'm assuming the group home didn't teach you."

Wow, the woman drove straight to the heart of the matter, didn't she? "No, when Demos recruited me, I was lacking in the sophistication I needed to blend in during certain missions. I think I took every protocol and etiquette lesson the man could drum up and then he sent me out with some of the more sophisticated amongst us to see if I'd pass muster. Let me tell you, I knew every fork, spoon, and knife before they sent me to the field. Where did you learn your manners?"

"I believe you've told me that I don't have manners." She took a small spoonful of caviar and topped her cracker.

He reached for the food but stopped. "I said that?"

"Hmm. Not in so many words, but there toward the end, before you stopped fighting the attraction between us, you were getting a bit testy."

He laughed. "Yeah, well, I had blue balls, big time, and I really, really didn't want to like you as much as I do."

In a very condescending tone, she asked, "Poor Smoke. Is the widdle girl such a problem?"

"Problem? No. Trouble? Oh hell, yeah." He made a plate of the offerings and leaned back in his chair. "When you landed on my boat all those nights ago, you warned me that you were trouble. I should have listened."

"Three months, twenty-four days ago to be exact, and hey, I have been damn good. I haven't gotten into any trouble since we paired up. That —" she pointed her butter knife at him "—is like a world record for me."

"Is that so?" He didn't believe it for a second. He didn't see troublemaker in her nature. She nodded as she popped an entire cracker loaded with caviar into her mouth. "So, what kind of trouble do you usually get into?"

"Oh, Lord above, what doesn't happen? I was in a bar once that was raided and I was arrested for prostitution."

He stopped chewing and turned his head to stare at her. "What?"

"No shit. The guy I was talking to was a cop. He put handcuffs on me and dragged me down to the station. It was a mess, but since I hadn't actually propositioned the guy yet, he had to let me go. He was wearing a wire and couldn't fake it."

Yet? What? "Proposition him as in ask him to pay you for sex?"

"Well, yeah, that's what prostitution is, you know. But he didn't have the evidence so that was a moot point."

He held up a hand. "No, hold on. Go back. You said '*yet*'. Explain yet."

"Oh, I had gotten into a fight, some asshole tried to slip something into my drink, I called him on it, and he tried to get away. I followed him out into the alley and the fucker had the balls to swing at me. Well, that didn't end well for him. I've taken down bigger assholes who were a lot more skilled." She took a sip of her whiskey and loaded up another cracker.

He waited while she finished her bite, but when she made no attempt to explain, he prompted her, "How does that equate to turning tricks at a bar?"

"What? Oh, well, the fucker in the alley had a partner. While I beat him down, she grabbed my purse and bolted. I had no money, no identification, no cell phone, no way of calling for help, and when you're in a foreign country, you need those things. I was one hell of a long way from the embassy, so I needed to think on my feet. I was going to get the guy alone and then jack him for whatever cash he had." She swallowed the rest of her drink and arched an eyebrow. "What did you think I was going to do?"

He slowly shook his head from side to side. "I honestly have no words right now."

"Meh, that's just the tip of the iceberg." She waved her hand. "Speaking of icebergs, when I went to Antarctica I almost froze to death."

He gave up any pretense of eating and leaned forward. "Antarctica?"

"Yeah, that continent way down south?"

"I know where it is. Why on earth would you want to go to Antarctica?"

"Dude, really? Because I could! The peninsula is absolutely phenomenal. The Lemaire Channel and Paradise Harbor have freaking icebergs on each side as you sail in. Besides, penguins! What else do you need to say?"

"How did you almost freeze to death?"

She pointed at him with half a roasted pecan. "That wasn't as difficult as you'd think."

"Well, Antarctica is known to be cold."

"Bingo. Anyway, I wanted to see what was over the hill. The tour went right, I turned left, and by the time I got done exploring, I was totally screwed up as to which way I needed to go to get back to the tour. Did you know every direction is freaking north down there?"

"One would assume." He chuckled when she rolled her eyes at him.

"Yeah, well, add all that into the bar fights, there was that fire—but I didn't cause it —then the car thing." Her eyebrows drew together. "I don't know how in the hell I ended up in a chop shop. I was just looking for a part for my dad's vintage car, you know? A friend of a friend said that I could get it from these guys, that they could get anything. So... yeah, that was fun."

He snapped his mouth shut and worked his way through those words. "No wonder they put you out in the middle of the ocean."

"Har, har, har." She lifted her whiskey glass and stared at it. "Trouble finds me. I swear, minus the left turn in Antarctica, none of the trouble I've been in was actually my fault."

"Uh-huh." He doubted it. "Bar fights? Really?"

"Dude, I seriously can walk into a bar and a fight will erupt. One time in Madrid, I walked in and some guy punched me in the face. I was three feet inside the bar, not even two seconds."

"And you were arrested for being a victim?"

"Hell, no. If you were punched in the face, would you take it lying down? I didn't. I got up, found a bar stool, and broke it over the man's head. Then his friends got involved and the people I was with felt they had to defend my honor... Needless to say, with the repairs to the bar and the repair to me, it was an expensive night out." She tapped her front teeth. "Implants. The bastard broke them out."

He stared at her and then smiled. "You're pulling my leg right now, aren't you?"

"Nope." She reached over, took his whiskey glass from his hand, and drank the rest of it. "I've had a few adventures."

"But you're only twenty-two."

Charley snorted. "And? Does age really matter?"

"How could you have done so much in such little time?"

"I told you. I just walk into a place, and boom; the shit hits the fan."

"And because of all that you decided the best thing for you to do was to become an operative?"

She snorted. "No. I became an operative because it's who I am. I don't want a stupid desk job or want to be someone's wife, doting on kids—which are great as long as they are someone else's—or managing my husband's social calendar. I know what *this* job entails."

"Because of your relationship to the Kings." He nodded; of course, she did.

"And others. Demos for one. I've known him my entire life." She mimicked the guy's New York accent: "One doesn't choose to become an operative, young lady, the calling chooses you."

"You must have had one heck of a childhood." Sometimes he longed for the normalcy of a family. He never had it, and from what he'd learned since he'd joined Guardian, his brother Chris hadn't, either. Both were in prisons of their parents' fucked up expectations. He probably got the better shake from life, even with past events considered.

"I think it was pretty typical." She shrugged. "I, however, am very atypical, which is why I am sitting here in a towel, in a house that isn't mine, eating someone else's food, and planning on having wild sex on their bed."

"Is that right?"

"Yep."

"Need any company?"

"Need? No, I've been taking care of myself for

the last four months." Her brows lifted and she glared at him.

"I was an idiot." He dropped his head to the table with a resounding thunk.

She snorted a laugh and agreed, "Yeah, you were. Come upstairs and make it up to me."

He popped his head off the table and smiled. "Wild sex?"

"Wild, unbridled, crazy, hot, sweaty, fun, dirty… take your pick." She stood up and let her towel drop to the floor. She looked at the terrycloth and then at him. "Whoops." She turned on her heel and walked out of the kitchen.

He stood up, catching his borrowed boxers before they fell to his knees, and sprinted after her. Her peal of laughter as she flew up the stairs ahead of him echoed in the empty house. He almost caught her before she jumped onto the bed, but falling on top of her a second later was just fine with him.

"Want to play?" He pinned her with his legs and grabbed her ribs with his hands. Her shriek of surprise was soon drowned out by her laughter and then by her pleading for him to stop. He dropped on top of her and cradled her head with his hands. Her face was flushed, and her smile was free, happy, and too damn innocent to be in this line of work, no matter what she'd told him about her life to this point.

"What's wrong?" She looked up at him, her smile faded.

"You don't know the hardships of this life. The crushing weight of the jobs we do. I don't want to see the light inside you go out." She fought hard to deny her innocence, but he could see it in her lightheartedness.

She pushed his too-long hair away from his eyes and sighed. "I might not have done this job for long, but I assure you, I know the weight of the responsibility on your shoulders. I've seen the way it tears a person apart. I've witnessed people I love struggle with decisions, and I'm aware that when that responsibility becomes mine, it will affect me. Doing the right thing, for the right reason, to protect the lives of innocents and make this world a better place is a privilege. One that could cost me my life or perhaps my light as you call it, but that is a bridge I've yet to cross."

"There are some bridges you can't walk across twice." He'd traversed them and had the scars, both physical and mental, to prove it.

"I know." She lifted and kissed him. No longer

filled with laughter, the kiss morphed into an acknowledgement of sameness. No matter the age difference, they were alike. The need to see, do, and explore enticed them, but the driving force that colored their entire world was the absolute need for justice.

He feasted on her tanned, toned body. The experiences with a new lover were always exciting. Finding the exact way to drive them higher, to reach the pinnacle of sexual desire and hold them there as long as possible before crashing with them over the edge was a thrill, but it was different with Charley, wasn't it? She was his partner, his support system, and his responsibility. His.

He trailed his lips from her breast to her ribs and used his tongue to swirl down to her sex. He hadn't tasted her yet, and God, the thought of her at the back of his throat made his cock weep with want. Shouldering between her legs, he wrapped his hand around her thighs and pulled her closer to his mouth.

Sweet as honey and fucking irresistible. Her hands tangled in his hair as she tried to arch closer to him, but no. As demanding as she was, making her wait, building up her release satisfied something carnal inside him. He needed her to know he was in charge, that he'd give her what she needed when he deemed her ready. She'd had boys, now he'd show her what a man could do.

He devoured her, pushing her higher with alternating licks and small nibbles before he'd suck and torment her most sensitive flesh. He smiled in self-satisfaction when she tightened under him and her sex clamped in a climax that made her gasp. He kissed the inside of each thigh before he lifted over her.

Dark brown hair fanned around her in a halo. The rose of her cheeks was echoed down her throat and across her chest. He dipped down and took a rosebud at the peak of her breast into his mouth. She jolted and grabbed his arms. He worked each hard nipple over and over until her words became a nonsensical pleading.

He entered her and her heat consumed and wrapped around him. She moved up to meet each slow, languid thrust. He dropped his forehead to her shoulder and let himself feel the way their bodies joined, the way her fingers gripped his shoulders, and the way their breathing shattered the silence of the room. Each sensation built against the next, bringing him closer. Charley arched her back and she shattered around him.

The intensity of her climax snapped his control and he drove into her, sprinting toward his own release. He held her tight as he came. The intensity of his release lit a display of reds and whites behind his tightly shut eyes. Everything condensed to that moment in time, the most basic primal need detonating through him, and he embraced the feelings that filled him after the explosion.

His traitorous heart had found another to care for, another to protect, but this time it wasn't a sibling type of attachment. He rolled off her and cradled her as she snuggled close. No, this time he'd gone and hooked onto bigger emotions. Did he cut the line and let the emotion go or did he reel it in? He had a pretty good idea what the churning under the water of his psyche was going to turn out to be once he started to bring in that line. The question was if he did, what was he to do with the damn thing?

Smoke felt for the knife under his pillow, gripping it as his entire body tensed. He sensed Charley had done the same thing. The rub of metal against metal was distinct and the exact sound he recognized from when they'd pushed the shutter away from the front of the window earlier.

Smoke was out of the bed and lifted a hand for Charley to remain where she was and to be silent. The distinct sound of footsteps downstairs had her out of the bed and on the other side of the door in a flash.

"Don't have a heart attack, Smoke. It's just me," a deep baritone called up the stairway.

His eyes narrowed as he placed the voice. "Reaper, you asshole, aren't you supposed to be watching our bogies?"

"Yeah, so hurry up, will ya? I brought weapons. Figured you'd need them sooner rather than later since all your shit got blown up."

"Stand by." Smoke motioned into the room. "Better put some clothes on and then come down. I'll introduce you."

Charley pushed her hair out of her face. She whispered, "You know him?"

"I do." Smoke moved to grab the boxers that were too big and put them on. He paused to look at her. "You coming?"

She shook her head and slid back into the bed. "You go. One of us has to be alert tomorrow and neither of us will be if we both go downstairs."

Smoke dropped onto the bed, slid the fall of dark brown hair from her neck, and dropped a kiss on her warm skin. "Did I wear you out?"

She chuckled, "Not ever going to get me to admit it. Let me go to sleep and I'll wear you out the next time."

"That's a deal." He chuckled and lifted the sheet over her stretch of beautifully exposed skin.

He padded downstairs and found Reaper at the liquor cabinet. The man turned and nodded to a small canvas tote. "I had duplicates in my traveling arsenal and Phoenix had a couple of things for you, too.

"I thought you were running solo?" Smoke moved to the bag and pulled out a forty-five, a nine mil, ammo, and a pleasant surprise. "Det Cord, C4, and blasting caps? You carry this on the routine?"

"Nah, that was Phoenix's gift. You know him. Fires and shit." Reaper dropped into one of the chairs and chuckled. "Didn't think to bring clothes."

"No worries, I can look like a grandpa tourist until Alpha's care package arrives." He grabbed a bottle of water out of the fridge and drank half of it. "What do you know about who targeted us?"

"Not much. Phoenix is watching the address these phones are congregated at. He'd rather just torch the place, and I can't say I'd have a different opinion. Fuckers nuked your boat, man."

"Ship, and yeah, that wasn't great to watch. Unfortunately, the mission is bigger than my revenge, otherwise, I'd help that crazy pyro light the match. Have you gotten the brief?" Smoke sat down and rubbed his neck.

"Nope. Just watching the blips. We were told the bogies may be in the same line of work we are."

"That's it in a nutshell. The one in charge needs to be positively ID'd before we take him out. The only thing is we don't know who he is."

Reaper stared at him and then shook his head. "That is a classic *Catch 22* situation, isn't it?"

He nodded and glanced at the window that they'd come through. "It is. You came in from the west?"

"Not my first rodeo, Smoke." The man crossed his arms.

"Not saying it is, but I have a partner and shit I'd tolerate before, I can't now."

"Sage is back?" Reaper sat up straighter. "Where the fuck is he, man?"

"No. My partner is someone else. Charley."

"Don't know him."

"New. A kid. Twenty-two."

"Ah, well, that explains not taking chances."

"Don't get me wrong, Charley is smart and well trained, but..."

"I get you, my man. Experience teaches lessons you can't learn any other way." Reaper stood up and rolled his shoulders. "I need to get back before Phoenix decides he should watch some flames dance. My mission is to fade into nothing when you hit Georgetown. I'll be around, but I can't be too close. I'm... recognizable."

"Ha. Funny." Smoke flipped his friend the finger.

Reaper looked at him and a smile crawled across his face. "I wasn't being a smartass on purpose. I meant I stand out in a crowd because of my size, not recognizable like your movie star face."

"Phoenix isn't supposed to be here, is he?" Smoke asked as Reaper headed toward the open window.

"No, but the monkey is on his back—hard. Since that last mission, he's been on a hair-trigger. Better if I keep an eye on him."

Smoke put a hand on Reaper's shoulder, halting

his climb out of the window. "Has he passed his Go/No Go evaluation?"

"Didn't ask and I don't care. He's saved my ass; I'll do what I can to save him, whether his presence is sanctioned or not. Whatever it takes, my man."

"As long as it takes, my friend."

He stuck out his hand and Reaper gripped it. "I'll be as close as I can be without endangering your mission."

"And I'm damn glad that you and Phoenix have my six."

He watched the Assassin drop down and move away into the darkness. He slid the shutter back and closed the window, setting his half-empty bottle of water against the ledge before he grabbed the weapons, ammo, and party tricks Reaper had brought them. Carrying that iron upstairs made him a bit more comfortable. The C4? Well, that was a security blanket. He drew a breath and headed up the stairs. Maybe he could get some sleep now.

CHAPTER 8

"Over there." Charley pointed to a parking slot and Smoke pulled in.

"What are we doing here?"

"I have money in that bank." She pointed in the direction of the largest bank on Grand Cayman. The sundress was chafing where she'd cinched it at the waist and she still had huge folds of fabric that she pinched under her arms to keep the front from flopping open. The woman who she borrowed the clothes from had to be a triple D cup and her B+ wasn't doing the job. She needed clothes—now.

"I think you're forgetting you don't have any identification." Smoke put the car in park and leaned back against the seat.

"I don't need it."

He blinked at her. "Say what now? They're going to let you in there and what, say, here, take our money?"

Charley rolled her eyes. "Just stay here. I'll be back and then we're getting clothes, food, and ditching this car."

"I think I'd rather come in with you." He turned off the vehicle and stared at her.

"Whatever." She'd manage somehow.

They looked ridiculous in the ill-fitting clothes, but they fit in better than they did wearing wetsuits.

Charley walked past the guard, who gave them both a lingering stare. She clutched her borrowed purse with her knife and nine mil to her side and walked up to the pedestal counter. She grabbed a pen and scribbled a note. She folded it in half and stepped away from the pedestal.

"Um, Charley, hate to tell you this, but there isn't any teller in this bank."

She turned and smiled at him. "Not that kind of bank, Dan."

He lifted an eyebrow and then turned his head toward the sound of high heels clicking against the marble flooring. Charley handed the woman her note and watched as she gazed at it. Yes, the double-take the woman gave her was expected and so was the immediate response.

"Right this way." They followed her into an opulent office, styled in minimalistic chrome and glass. The woman sat down and punched in a series of numbers. She handed Charley a keypad and she punched in a long series of numbers that she'd memorized many, many years ago, followed by the amount she wanted.

"Cash?" The woman asked but didn't look at either of them when she asked.

Charley sighed as if she was bored. "Half."

"Digital access for the remainder?"

"Of course." She glanced at Smoke.

His eyes traveled around the office, to the door, back to the woman. He wasn't comfortable, rather he felt uneasy for some reason.

She scanned the office again and then looked at the door. There were three men congregated at the center of the huge lobby. The guard pointed to the office where they were seated.

Damn it. Of course, this would happen. She sighed and put a hand on Smoke's arm and gave him a smile.

"I'll be back momentarily." The woman stood

and straightened her pencil skirt before she exited the office.

"Who are they?" Smoke asked as soon as the glass door shut.

"I'd wager they are the bank officers."

"Why are they talking to our teller?" His eyes were glued to the men. His muscles were tight, and he was ready to react.

"Because I have a lot of money in this bank."

"You do?" Smoke glanced around.

She smiled and leaned forward. Her sundress popped open and she grabbed at the material, shoving it under her arm again, pinning the excess fabric to her side. "Damn it, this dress. I'll go out and deal with them. Really, I hate this damn thing. I hate dresses. Period." She stood up and left before he could argue.

Charley walked up to the men as they moved toward her, their serious faces not at all welcoming. She cocked her head. "Is there a problem, gentlemen? I was assured my money was secure at this establishment. Do I need to call my lawyers?"

"No, not at all," the eldest of the three spoke after the younger two glanced at him.

"I provided the code and the proper pin. Are

you requesting further identification, which I believe is in direct violation of your own statutes?"

"No, ma'am, it is just rare that one of our primary accounts visits us in person. We wanted to extend all our services to you. We couldn't help but notice..."

The man's voice trailed off and she chuckled. "My clothes? Yes, a series of unfortunate happenings, to be sure."

"Would you like us to arrange for anything while you are on the island, Ms.—"

She held up her hand. "Not necessary. Thank you. Now, I must return to my traveling companion before he convinces himself that I'm being accosted. He's rather protective." She glanced over her shoulder at Smoke, who stood outside the office door with his arms crossed over his chest. The man wore a resting bitch face that his pansy-assed brother couldn't mimic for all the money in Hollywood.

"Is that..."

She turned and again held up a hand. "Gentlemen, decorum, please." The men harrumphed and pulled on their suit jackets, straightening away imaginary creases. "I'll be sure to let him know how kind you've been. Perhaps he'd be interested in an account with you."

She could see the greed dripping off all three of them. Smoke's brother was one of the highest-paid actors in the world. The oldest of the three bank officers reached out, took her hand, and bowed over it. "It is our pleasure to have you on the premises. Anything we can do to make your stay in Grand Cayman more pleasurable, do not hesitate to reach out to us." A thick linen card appeared with only a telephone number on it. She smiled nicely in an extremely uninterested way; the same smile she'd seen her mother conjure countless times. She turned and walked away as gracefully as she could in the too-big sandals. To seal her cover, when she reached Smoke, she leaned up to kiss him. The frown on his forehead didn't lessen. "What did they want?"

"Long, long story. Let's just get the money and get out of here. I need clothes that fit, you need a hat and sunglasses, and we both need food." She opened the door and dropped back into the chair, waiting for her 'teller' to bring the cash and bank card.

"I have a feeling you aren't telling me everything." He plopped down in his chair after he repositioned it so he could better see the foyer area of the establishment.

"If I could..." She let the sentence trail off. Would she? Would she really tell him her secrets? Would she reveal everything to him and watch him scamper away? Or worse, have him change the way he treated her? No. Probably not, and the reason for not telling him was a double-edged sword. She liked him. The last four months, they'd danced around the attraction they had while they did minor little jobs for Guardian. But since he'd opened up to her and she'd been able to fill in the many blanks in her knowledge of Dan Collins, she'd realized that it wasn't just a sexual relationship she wanted.

And. That. Was. Bad.

Any hopes of a real relationship were doomed. She'd kept in front of the shitstorm heading her way and she'd never felt freer, but sooner or later, she'd have to pay the piper and deal with the things she'd done. The deception and manipulation that she'd pulled others into and the responsibility of decisions she'd made was on her and her alone.

Smoke had talked about not knowing the

weight of the responsibilities of the profession. Well, she knew the responsibility of making decisions, ones that gave her freedom and a life away from the controlling environment of her past. She knew well the consequences of those decisions and still, she'd make every move over again. There was no question about it. She'd want to end up here, today, with… She glanced over at Smoke.

He was leaning forward, keeping his eyes on the foyer. He lifted suddenly and nodded. "Here she comes."

They walked out of the bank five minutes later with a bank card and her oversized bag stuffed with low denominations. They stopped at the car, Smoke retrieved the bag of explosives, and while she blocked the view, he snugged his ad hoc belt a bit tighter and readjusted his weapon.

"I really hope you don't shoot yourself in the ass," she sniggered as he shoved his weapon between his belt and his back.

He whipped his eyes up to her. "Now, why would you say something like that? What did I say about negative vibes?"

She couldn't help it; she threw back her head and laughed. "Do you honestly believe because I said it it's going to happen?"

"I believe that what you said sits up here—" he pointed to his head "—and putting that type of thought in anyone's brain is wrong."

"You'll just have to be more careful." She slammed the trunk closed.

He lifted his small, canvas tote bag. "This is what I'm comfortable with. What's tucked under my belt, I use proficiently."

She glanced down at his fly and lifted her eyes slowly. "Yes, very proficient, I'd say." The red behind his deep tan was impossible to miss. "Are you blushing?"

"The bane of having a light complexion." He grabbed her elbow and hustled her down the street.

"You don't have a light complexion." She laughed at him as he rolled his eyes. She glanced around. "Where are you marching me to, sir?"

"I have no idea." He stopped and looked around. "Clothes and food, right?"

"Yes, and both are in this direction." She tugged him in the opposite direction he'd been hot-footing her. "We don't want to go that way. The cruise terminal is that way. This is the more exclusive part of Georgetown."

"How do you know that?" Smoke strolled alongside her. "I need sunglasses and a hat."

"I know. We'll get those first."

Two hours later, they casually walked along the street near the hotel they'd be surveilling. They found an outside bistro table across the street and down a couple hundred feet. When the waitress approached, they ordered a soft drink and settled in. Charley saw him as soon as he emerged onto the street from the alleyway. A dangerous man. Menace radiated off him as he prowled closer. His black hair, dark eyes, square chin, and sculpted muscles made for a beautiful man, but underneath that remarkable attractiveness was evil. Pure, unadulterated evil. She reached into her purse and flipped the safety off her nine mil. It would probably take her entire clip to put the stone wall of a man on his knees, but Smoke would have her six. Not once did the guy's eyes land on her or the table. They were fixed straight ahead, but as he passed, a cell phone and a note slid onto the table. The movement was casual, and if she hadn't been watching, she wouldn't have known the man had deposited them.

Smoke chuckled and picked up his drink. "Reaper is hard to miss, isn't he?"

"He's… intense."

"I'm glad he's on my side, I've seen him work, and intense is the understatement of the millennia." Smoke picked up the Guardian cell phone and pocketed it. "What's it say?" He nodded to the note. He swallowed hard and turned his stare to the building they were watching. Until this second, she'd forgotten he couldn't read without a struggle. So, obviously, Reaper didn't know Smoke's secret either, or he'd have communicated some other way. She took a drink of her soda and covered the note with her napkin, sliding it to her lap. She glanced down.

"Two of the phones are still inside. One left about three hours ago. P is on the rover." She leaned back in her chair, unable to see the building without turning. "Who is P?"

"Phoenix."

"Ah, I thought only one asset was here with us."

"It appears there are two." Smoke shrugged. "Sometimes, being near someone who understands the darkness helps."

She nodded. She wouldn't know, but it made sense.

The phone in his pocket vibrated. Smoke pulled it out and glanced at the face before he handed it to her. She glanced at the face and swiped it to open the thing. "It's locked." She glanced up at him.

"Try zero, one, one, zero." He watched as she keyed it in.

"How did you know?"

"We've used the code before in previous ops. It was an assumption." He shrugged.

"You support a lot of the…" she glanced around before she continued "people in your line of work, don't you?"

"My specialty is used primarily for clean-up or perhaps a deny and defend op. Every now and then, I get handed a mission like this one where I'm primary." He whispered his reply. She had to lean forward to hear him.

"Does that bother you?"

He shook his head. "I'm useful. I have people over me that I trust absolutely. My ego isn't bruised by being second seat in an operation. Teamwork isn't a bad thing."

"But because you're so easily confused with your brother, they limit your interaction on land."

"Bingo. What was the message?"

She glanced down. A cold chill tripped over her skin as she read the message. "Rover incapacitated. P."

"Shit. He wasn't supposed to make contact." Smoke dropped his head into his hand and then whipped it back up to keep eyes on the hotel doorway.

"Ask him where and the status of Rover."

She typed in the words and hit send. A text came back almost immediately. "GS to gut. Not me. Interrogating."

"Fuck." Smoke said the words almost to himself.

She looked up at him. "What?"

He shook his head. "There won't be much left of the man after Phoenix gets done with him."

"What if he's our man?"

"Text him to get a DNA sample." Smoke nodded to the phone. She punched in the words and hit send and the phone beeped in her hand. Her eyes darted up to him.

"The other two are on the move." They watched the front of the building. A man and woman exited, followed by two men.

"Which ones?" she asked him.

"I've got the men, you take the couple. We follow, gather intel only."

"You don't have any comms," she hissed the words as he stood.

"Not a worry, I'm not contacting them, remember?"

"Right. Where do we meet up?"

He swiveled his head and nodded across the street. "There. Neither leaves that bar unless we are together."

She nodded and dropped money onto the table for their drinks. "See you later. Be careful."

"That's my line to you." He touched the bill of his new Grand Cayman ball cap and followed the two men at a distance. She walked past the couple she was following and turned to window-shop, getting a good look at both of them. The woman was clothed in designer labels and her fingers dripped with diamonds. Her nails were extremely long and decorated in crystals with charms looped off the end of the ring fingers. The man, on the other hand, didn't appear to be enamored with the woman. She was clingy, and although he was tolerant, there was an air about him that told her he'd rather be anywhere else. Was this his wife or mistress? His frequent glances at his watch betrayed his boredom. The woman pulled him into a specialty purse shop and Charley entered the store across the street where she admired a pair of heels. "Can I help you?"

The woman's voice behind her diverted her attention for a second. She gave the woman a quick glance. "No, thank you." She pointed to the store across the street. "I'm following my husband and his mistress."

"Oh." The saleslady came and stood next to her. "Are you getting pictures?"

"Dang, I hadn't thought about that. Do you think anyone would see me?" She glanced around, looking as helpless as she could.

"Maybe. If you give me your phone, I'll take them. I can step outside and take a picture and they'd never know I'm using your phone."

"Would you mind?"

"Not at all. I loathe cheating scumbags. I was married to one. Twice."

"Twice?" She did a double-take at the saleswoman.

"Yep. What can I say, he is damn good in bed."

Charley sighed, "My husband isn't, maybe that's

why he has to buy her all the jewelry and gifts, huh?"

The saleswoman chortled and then held out her hand. "Is that them?"

"Yep." Charley opened the phone and turned on the camera so the woman couldn't see anything else on the phone.

The woman exited the store while Charley moved to the side to watch both the couple and the woman with her phone. It took less than thirty seconds and the woman was back. "There you go. I even got one of her kissing him, because sweetie, he looked like he wanted to crawl away. But any court in the world will take one look at that and back your petition."

Charley chuckled. "Thanks. I'm going to see where else they go."

"Good luck, and take that man for all he's worth."

Charley waved and exited the store. She kept an eye on the couple by sitting on a park bench as they moved in and out a row of specialty stores. While they worked their way down the avenue, she called Guardian.

"Operator Two Seven Four. Good Afternoon, Sunset Operative Seventeen."

"Nope, this is Thorn Twenty-two. Send me to CCS, please."

"CCS," Bengal's voice answered the phone.

"Hey, Smoke and I were split up. I'm following a couple on a shopping excursion. Where are the bogies?"

She heard Bengal cover the phone and ask a question. He returned and replied, "Seven Mile Beach."

"Shit, I'll head back toward them."

"The third bogey is concerning."

"Yeah, he was shot," Charley informed Bengal.

"Repeat last?" The acidic response made her butt cheeks clench.

She closed her eyes and spoke. "The person following them texted us and told us he'd been gut shot. Our person was not the shooter. He is, however, trying to extract information. We requested DNA."

There was complete silence on the phone for several long seconds. "Reunite with Smoke. Check in every thirty minutes until you're together again."

"For fuck's sake, I'm not two."

"Thorn Operative Twenty-Two, that is an

order," Bengal's voice snapped over the connection.

"Copy all." Charley ended the call and out of habit deleted the call from the phone's memory. She stood up and turned toward Seven Mile Beach. That's when the woman she'd been watching stepped in front of her. Charley spun, but too late. The barrel of the weapon dug into her back. "Hey, what's going on?"

The man whispered in her ear, "You are very stupid for an operative, aren't you?"

She tried to turn again, but the barrel of the weapon dug deeper, making her hiss. "What are you talking about?"

"The photographs of you on the boat were more revealing than the clothes you are wearing now."

"I really don't know what you're talking about."

"Your tune will change once Dahlia here has a chance to work on you." The woman in front of her smiled and her eyes ran up and down Charley like a starving dog looking at a side of beef. The woman wore heels which she didn't need; she was tall and lanky in a loose-boned kind of way

"You've got the wrong person." Boy did they. The woman who'd helped her out came out of the little shoe shop and crossed her arms, looking at them.

"Move."

Charley kept her feet firmly on the concrete of the sidewalk. The man shoved her and the woman from the shoe shop yelled across the street, "Hey! You! Leave her alone!"

Both of her new best friends looked at the woman. Charley spun, bumping into the man, trapping the weapon between them. She gripped his wrist to keep the weapon pointed up and kneed the man's elbow, using his radius and ulna as a spike to strike the gun up, putting the barrel just under his chin. She slipped her hand over his, pinning both of their fingers into the trigger guard. One wrong move and the man's brain was cement paint. It was a move she'd learned from her father many years ago and it worked every time. She pivoted, pulling the man off balance and down, putting him between Mistress Cat Claws and her. "This thing goes off and you lose your head. Call off your mistress and we both walk away alive."

"Dahlia, back off." The woman's eyes narrowed but she didn't move.

"You want his head blown off, sister? You got it."

"I called the police!" The saleslady yelled from across the street.

Charley pinned Dahlia with a stare and smiled. "Did you come in through customs, sweetheart? Bet you'll have a devil of a time explaining how you got here, otherwise." The man tried to move, but she shoved the gun deep into the flesh under his chin. "Stop moving, I may squeeze the trigger, fuckwad. Wait, what am I saying? Please, keep moving. I can just see your brain matter all over your girlfriend there. She'd look lovely."

The wailing of sirens in the distance jolted the woman out of her bravado. She turned on her heel and racewalked in those heels, leaving her lover with Charley. "Wow, how is that for the fickle face of love?" Charley asked the man. "Now, slip your hand out from under mine. Slowly." She watched the scenarios float across the man's brain as if she was inside looking out. There wasn't an out. He couldn't leave any other way and she'd kill him if he made one wrong move. His hand relaxed and he slipped it out of the trigger guard. She lowered the weapon and they stepped back as if on some silent count only they could hear.

As the sirens neared, he spun and raced away. The saleswoman jogged across the street as Charley placed her newly acquired weapon in her purse, out of the woman's view. "I really didn't call the police. I didn't want to cause you any more trouble, but those sirens came in handy, didn't they?"

Charley hugged the woman. "Thank you so much. I don't know how they snuck up on me." And that was the truth. She stared at the bank of stores across the street from her.

"Oh, there is a small walkway that goes from the back side of these stores around this way. They cross at that intersection and it comes out there." She pointed to a walkway behind the bench she was sitting on.

Well, that explained how they were able to get the drop on her, and it also told her that maybe the couple knew the ins and outs of the island… but they weren't the ones she was *supposed* to be tracking. At least, they weren't the ones that had been at the house. She thanked the saleswoman again and headed back the way she'd come with one eye on her six and the other eye forward. She was being watched, of that, there was no doubt, so instead of going to Seven Mile Beach to find her partner, she was heading back to the small tavern where they'd agreed to meet. *Because what could go wrong with her in a bar? Right?* She gritted her teeth. For once, she was hoping whatever trickster God juju she attracted stayed the fuck out of sight. She would find a seat, plant her ass with her back against a wall, and she'd wait for Smoke. *Quietly*.

CHAPTER 9

Smoke stalked down the street, his head tucked and his ball cap pulled low. He put out his best 'don't fuck with me' vibe. Because it *was* a vibe, no matter what Charley thought; they radiated around people. For the most part, his 'don't fuck with me' vibe kept people from approaching if they *thought* he might be Chris.

The two men he'd followed had wandered Georgetown in no particular hurry to go anywhere and even spent two hours in the sea turtle sanctuary. The fact that another member of their little cabal had been taken out wasn't known—*or* they really didn't give a fuck. He glanced right and left then hot-footed it across the intersection, making it back to the street where they started this morning. This time, Smoke was leading them, checking at random intervals to ensure they hadn't made a detour, but now, it was obvious they were heading back to the hotel. The entire day had been a major bust. He had picked up a pay-as-you-go cell phone and provided the number to Guardian. There had been no calls and no updates. It was a fucking waste of a day, but he'd be lying to himself if he didn't feel the thrill of actually *doing* something.

Of course, with his ship gone, he was strapped to the land. Hopefully, he could find another drug king who liked to sail. There had to be at least one or two of them left in the world. Either that or he'd buy his own. He had money tucked in offshore accounts all over the world. He'd had Valkyrie invest a hefty chunk about five years ago. That assassin made money hand over fist and had put him in the extremely rich category. She had brains behind the beauty and was an ice-cold killer, through and through. He'd blown the shit out of a building to provide her an emergency exit strategy when she was first starting out and she'd never forgotten. Hell, he tried to explain to her that was why he was there. His wasn't a singular calling anymore, although he spent more time alone than any of the others combined. Well, except for

Tempest. That man was locked in solitary for years. Now as a part of a Thorn Team he was considered a regular operative with special skills.

He slowed and then sat down in one of the bistro seats at the small cafe where they'd started the surveillance this morning. The two he'd been following crossed the street and entered the hotel. He texted Guardian:

> *Bogey in the hole*

That would let them know the two were back in the hotel.

> *Reaper on. 1830. Thorn Team.*

Guardian's reply added a question mark at the end of the day, but Reaper would cover the hotel so he could meet with Charley, and they'd make a call to Guardian at six-thirty as directed. Hopefully, for a better game plan. He'd been considering the options all day as he wandered Georgetown and avoided the stares of tourists. He'd settled on the idea that they could take the duo the next time they stepped out of the hotel and let Phoenix work on them. As the assassin had said on more than one occasion, fire was an amazing conversation starter.

He got up from the table and left a tip for the privilege of occupying the space before he headed to the small tavern where he'd told Charley to meet him.

He closed one eye behind his sunglasses. When he entered the darker area, he'd switch open eyes so he could immediately see in the darkness. A little trick that had saved his ass more than once. He stepped into the interior and immediately ducked to the side, just missing being hit in the face with a bar stool. The wood shattered, nicking his arm. Instinctively, he moved into a crouch, waiting for the next attack. Instead… *Shit.*

There was a major fight in progress. Almost everyone in the bar was involved.

"What the…" His head whipped around, taking in any imminent threats, but he was relatively safe. However, right in the middle of the fray was Charley. *Holy hell.* She threw a right hook and downed a man three times her size. Another man lifted a barstool behind her.

"Charley, your six!"

Without missing a beat, she dropped and swept behind her with her leg and sent the man down on his ass, the stool landed on top of his head, and he fell backward like a bag of cement. She snapped her attention back to Smoke and yelled, "Duck!"

He dipped and avoided the sucker punch coming his way. Lifting up, he added a left uppercut to his momentum and struck home on the asshole's jaw. The asshole's head snapped backward, but Smoke grabbed the fucker's head and rammed it into his knee as he lifted it, sending the man onto the floor in an unconscious flop.

Another man grabbed Charley from behind. Smoke made it three steps before someone else got in his way. The fucker lasted two hard punches before Smoke could move forward. He had to get to Charley. Some asshole was using her as a punching bag now that she was being held from behind. Smoke launched himself and dove at the man's knees, knocking him into Charley and the person holding her, dropping all of them to the floor.

He sucked at wrestling, but it was the only

chance he had to break the other fucker's hold on Charley and take out the bastard bagging on a woman. The fucker under him snapped his head back and landed a perfect blow to Charley's nose. He kneed the man in the back and wrenched his arm so high he heard the shoulder pop. The man screamed and Charley cussed. A pair of size thirteen shitkickers registered next to him along with the disappearing legs of a barstool.

Fuck. That word was the limit of his mental ability to process. *Fuck. Oh, fuck.* There was a hydraulic drill boring a hole through his brain. He blinked his eyes open and slowly turned to see where he was. Bars. "Wonderful."

He sat up and gave himself a minute to stop spinning before he opened his eyes again. He was in a cell by himself, and across the hall… was Charley. He blinked and stared at her. What was that hanging… *Oh.*

Two bloody, twisted pieces of tissue stuck out her nose. She lifted a hand. "I see you're alive."

"Barely. What the fuck, Charley?"

She sighed, "I swear I was minding my own business."

Smoke closed one eye so he could keep her in focus better. Yeah, he probably had a concussion, but he'd have to deal. He cleared his throat and closed his eyes for a moment. "Our circumstances would lead me to believe otherwise. Where are the men who were beating the shit out of you?"

"I don't know. I don't think the cops arrested them. And they were *trying* to beat the shit out of me. I held my own pretty well. Dan, they had a girl, she couldn't have been fourteen, and they were touching her… inappropriately. She was scared. I could see it, and there were four of them… I had to do something." She dropped her head back against the wall.

"What happened to her?"

"When I interrupted, she bit the guy holding her and hightailed it out the front door. Hopefully, she got away. I told her to go get the police."

"I think she found them. How are you feeling?" He leaned back on his cot and mimicked her position.

"I think my nose is broken, a couple bruised ribs, and my hand will be swollen for a hell of a long time." She lifted up her right hand; the knuckles were bruised and scraped. Yeah, his partner was a fucking brawler, wasn't she?

He looked at his wrist. His watch was missing. Naturally. He'd liked that dive watch, damn it. "What time is it?"

"I have no idea. It's dark." She pointed to a window over his head.

Yeah, no, he wasn't going to crank his head and neck around to see. "We were supposed to check in at six-thirty."

"I'd say we missed that check-in."

"No doubt."

The sound of a key in a lock sat them both upright on their cots.

Reaper sauntered into the cell area, twirling the keys around his index finger. "So, why do you get to have all the fun?" He unlocked the cell door and opened it.

Smoke stood and headed toward his friend. "For the record, I'm *not* having fun." He pointed to Charley's cell. "My partner, if you please?"

Reaper cocked his head and examined Charley. "Bet you're pretty when you don't have tampons hanging out of your nose."

"Bet you're a gigantic asshole even when you

don't have that smug look on your face," Charley snipped back.

Reaper threw back his head and laughed. "I so am." He unlocked the door and swung it open. He tossed the keys in the air and reached into his pocket. "Yours. I recognized it on the way in. I think the jailer took a liking to it."

"Is this a jailbreak?" Smoke asked as he strapped on his watch.

"Nah… well, not really. This isn't the jail; it's more like a holding area. The dork outside fell asleep compliments of a little knockout juice on a rag. He's sleeping soundly. When he wakes up, you'll be gone."

"Did Guardian send you?" Charley headed out the door Reaper came in.

"It wasn't Avon, sweetheart. Did they book you? Prints, pictures, anything?" Reaper pointed to a wall of file cabinets and the computer.

"No, it was more like a drunk tank toss," Charley answered.

Reaper's eyebrows lifted. "So, you have experience with drunk tanks?"

"More than you'd think," Smoke answered for Charley, who was carefully extracting the twisted tissue from her nostrils.

She chucked them in the garbage can and shrugged. “Shit happens.”

“To you,” Smoke mumbled.

“Weapons?” Reaper asked before they left.

“Mine was left in my purse at the bar. I pulled his weapon and hid it under the bar when it was obvious the cops were there to toss us, not the regulars.”

Smoke, Charley, and Reaper walked out into the dark. Glancing at his analog watch, he sighed. “We need to check in. Today was a total bust.”

“No, it wasn't,” both Charley and Reaper answered at the same time.

Smoke got into the vehicle indicated.

“The couple I followed tried to turn the tables. Thanks to an attentive saleslady, I was able to slip out of their grasp. Dahlia is the only name I got, but she's the one they were going to have work me over. I really want to meet her again. I have a good description of both of them. The only thing is that man, I didn't get an assassin vibe off him. Or her for that matter, but I'd think she'd be more capable of taking the headshot than he would.”

“The two I watched were a bust.” Smoke glanced over at Reaper. “What was Phoenix able to find out?”

"Don't know everything. He was talking to Anubis when I was sent to find you two." Reaper's eyes kept scanning the streets. He turned and turned again, going one way first and then the other. Once he was satisfied he wasn't being followed, he drove about a mile to a small hotel. He handed over two key cards. "My secondary location, room seventeen. Phoenix is at the primary keeping eyes on the bogies." Smoke took the keys and opened the door, noticing that the dome light did not come on. Reaper put a hand on his arm. "I'm assuming you lost the Guardian phone." He produced another cell. "Alpha's package is coming in tomorrow morning. I'll pick it up and bring it here. You call in and get your head on straight, maybe take an aspirin or something. Fridge has food, whiskey is on the dresser, and the bathroom has the standard medical kit."

"Thanks, man." He took the phone and got out, offering a hand to Charley. Of course, she didn't take it and gutted out getting out of the car. Bruised ribs were a motherfucker to deal with because other than wrapping them, there was nothing you could do about them but let them heal.

The hotel room was remarkably unremarkable. A queen bed with a print spread that matched the drapes. A television on top of the dresser and a small fridge. A sealed bottle of whiskey was on the dresser by the television. He moved through the room and into the bathroom, checking for signs of someone tampering. There was still a small thread at the side of the medical cabinet that would float away unnoticed if someone had opened it. The refrigerator had the same precaution which was similarly undisturbed. He checked the lamps while Charley unscrewed the receiver of the phone and then put it back together. She unplugged the phone and turned it over, checking under the plating on the bottom. She gave him a thumbs-up and slowly laid down on the bed. He sat in the one and only chair so as not to jostle her and dialed Guardian, putting the phone on speaker.

"Operator Two Seven Four."

"Thorn Team Bravo reporting in."

"Stand by Thorn Team Bravo."

He glanced over at Charley; her eyes were closed, her mouth open because breathing out of her nose was probably a bitch right now. The woman had done the right thing but at the wrong time. They were going to fucking get kicked from this assignment. The crayon writing was on the wall.

"Authenticate Powder." Was that Anubis?

"Keg." He recited immediately.

"What the actual fuck, Smoke?" Yep, that was Anubis.

"Which actual fuck are we speaking of… you have to be specific," he chuckled despite his headache.

Anubis snapped, "This is not a joke, smartass."

He winced at the volume of Anubis' reply. "Yeah, chill, dude. I got that along with a fucking concussion, so yelling isn't going to help." The hydraulic drill was starting to speed up.

"What is your status?"

"Battered."

"Explain that in *finite* detail." Anubis' voice lowered. Oh yeah, one of his fearless leaders was pissed with a capital P.

"Charley saw four men accosting a young girl, as in not even legal. She stopped them, got the girl a chance to get to safety, and was taking on all four when I showed up for our rendezvous. A bar stool got the better of me after I took down two. Charley's nose is probably broken, her ribs are bruised, but she was going strong until that fucker hit her nose with the back of his head. I'm pretty certain I have a concussion from the bar stool breaking over my head and she's probably got a bitch of a headache, too."

Charley gave him a thumbs-up in acknowledgement.

Anubis sighed, "Are you able to continue on this mission? Dive? Mix in public without looking like a piece of shit?"

Charley's eyes opened and stared at him. She was letting him make the call. Breathing through her mouth wasn't going to be a problem, although maneuverability in the water with bruised ribs and the fit of the mask against the bridge of her nose would suck. She could probably hide the majority of her bruising with makeup.

"We can." He stared at her as he spoke.

"Stand by." The line went dead. He looked at the face of the phone; the call was still connected. He pointed at the phone and then lifted a finger to his lips, letting Charley know they were still connected. She simply closed her eyes. He stood and made his way into the bathroom with the phone in his hand. He opened the medicine cabinet and fished out a new box of over-the-counter painkillers. He sat the box on the nightstand beside her and headed for the whiskey bottle. He checked the seal and then opened it.

Charley had opened the box and unwrapped the top when he came back with the whiskey bottle. He handed it to her, and she popped two of the painkillers and followed it with a slug of whiskey. He popped two and washed them down with whiskey, too. Of course, there was a cursory thought given to his liver, but he'd always imagined he'd die before the damn thing could crap out on him.

"CCS online."

"Alpha online."

"The Rose online."

"The Annex online."

"Archangel online."

"Smoke, Anubis briefed us as to the circumstances today. To say I am unhappy about the blip on the locals' radar would be an understatement."

"It was my fault." Charley's voice sounded stronger than she looked right now.

"Thorn Operative Twenty-Two, you were not addressed. You want to be treated like one of my people, this is that. I'll address you if I need information from you. Smoke, you are the senior operative in charge. This entire mess is on you and on you alone."

"I understand, sir."

Charley sat up and hissed as her arms wrapped around her ribs. "What? Why in the hell?"

He held up a hand. "We'll discuss this after the call."

"Alpha," Archangel ground out.

"The care package will arrive tomorrow morning. Reaper will deliver it to you. In that package is a set of maps. I need you two to decipher the information we're sending and give us a game plan by tomorrow afternoon." Alpha's voice rang loud and clear into the room.

"Understood." Smoke was listening to the words not said. Words like 'removed from mission' or 'return to station'.

Alpha continued, "Sierra Team will arrive with the package. They will be taking over surveillance."

Charley motioned at him and mouthed, 'man and woman' to him.

He narrowed his eyes. 'They don't know?' he mouthed back.

With the tiniest movement, she shook her head. *Well, fuck him raw with a sandpaper-wrapped dildo.*

This was going to be fun. He cleared his throat. "We have some information to brief."

"The line is still secure," Bengal's wife spoke.

"Proceed," Archangel growled.

"There were four people who exited the hotel when you informed us of the bogies moving. I took two men who rambled around the city and did absolutely nothing of note. Charley, on the other hand, followed a man and a woman." He looked at her and nodded. She leaned forward and winced but gave her briefing quickly and succinctly.

"This happened after you contacted us?" Bengal's voice came over the line.

"Yes, immediately afterward," Charley acknowledged.

"And you failed to call it in." Archangel's voice dripped with condemnation.

"I didn't call it in because I wasn't in a private location," Charley stated.

There was a long minute of silence before Fury spoke, "What did the other asset uncover?"

Anubis cleared his throat and answered, "Our operative related the bogie he was following met with a man in a black Land Rover, the tag numbers provided come back as diplomatic plates. The passenger window rolled down and the man was shot twice, once to the stomach and once in the chest. The chest wound missed the heart, the bullet to the gut did irreparable damage."

Archangel rasped, "What country do the plates come back to?"

"The Honorary Consulate of Honduras." Anubis provided the information.

"And why would the Honduras delegation on Grand Cayman eliminate someone?" Alpha asked.

Smoke shook his head. "Sir, perhaps the question to ask is why would the Honduran Consulate have something to fear from Akuma?"

There was a long pause. "Oh, I like that question. Can I answer it? Please! I know the answer." Bengal's wife's voice overrode the sound of typing in the background.

"The floor is yours, Jewell." Archangel's voice softened a bit.

"Coolio. Here we go. The Consulate of Honduras in the Grand Cayman is the President of Honduras' little sister. Camelia and her husband Renaldo took up residence about seven months ago. The sister is the official, her husband is on Grand Cayman with her and is under diplomatic immunity, which is really, really good because

Spain has stated he is wanted for crimes against the Crown in their country."

"What crimes?" Fury asked.

"Funny you should ask. The majority of the information has been expunged, and very well, I might add, but there is traceable information ending in the Spanish warrants of not only Camelia and Renaldo but two South Korean citizens. The documents were signed and executed on the exact same day. Of course, their names have been redacted, but I worked some magic. The thing is, a search of the immigration department's records in South Korea indicate there are no active passports for the names given by the Spanish documents nor are there any records of those names departing the country, at least by legal means."

"It ties Camelia and Renaldo to South Korea, not North Korea," Jacob sighed.

"Oh, but wait, there's more!" Jewell laughed after her infomercial imitation. "I ran the name Renaldo Uribes through our databases. That name didn't hit, but Renaldo Castells did. Uribes is his wife's name. He took her name because of her brother's power. His actual last name is Castells and he popped on a very interesting list."

Both Smoke and Charley leaned forward as if the act would hurry Jewell's explanation. It didn't, and finally, Jason growled, "Which is?"

"Oh, right. Renaldo Uribes-slash-Castells is one of the senior players in Three's organization."

"Will that organization ever die?" Fury's cold words scratched across the connection.

"Hardly, they were infectious and are everywhere," Jason responded. "Can we prove this Renaldo Castells is the same person as Renaldo Uribes?"

"Wait," Smoke interrupted. "What difference does it make? It still doesn't tie this man to North Korea or the mission we're on."

Jason sighed and then spoke. "We know for a fact that Akuma worked for the Fates as an insurance policy upon their untimely death and we've found information in the Fates' computer documentation that they had used Darryl Clayborne's assassins for more than one hit. Several, it would seem, of very prominent political officials."

Smoke leaned in and asked, "Excuse me, sir, but I still don't see how these circumstances tie to our mission."

Charley looked up at him. "Succession? In Stratus?"

"Yes, if Renaldo is the same man who was upper management in Three's organization, he could have reached out to Akuma," Alpha mused.

Smoke shook his head, but Alpha beat him to the punch and added, "Only to kill their representative. That doesn't make sense."

"Unless Renaldo is sending a message," Fury interjected. "Fuck with me and I'll take you down. Start out strong. Is Clayborne going to wage war over one foot soldier or is he going to strike an agreement, one benefiting both of them? There's no other reason for him to be on Grand Cayman other than a meeting. Clayborne is safe in North Korea. If he was pulled to the island to conduct this parlay, he'd send minions first. I would. His next step is to make a statement. My next act would be to have those working for me storm the consulate and secure Renaldo and Camelia. Then, if I ran the organization, I would be visiting the man who took out one of my assets."

"Vengeance?" Archangel asked.

"Business," Fury replied. "He wants Renaldo's money, but he needs the man's fear and, to a degree, respect. He doesn't want to be a dog on a leash. Clayborne wants to be you."

"Me?" Archangel's question reverberated in the sudden silence.

Fury snorted. "He wants power. You can tell by the way he is outsourcing ad hoc jobs, and if he's here, he's shopping for more. Otherwise, he'd be in North Korea living life large with the government's backing."

"So, you think he's trying to grow his organization and Renaldo is the next step?" Anubis asked.

"I do. Logically, it makes sense. Jewell, send me a list of what other upper-level players of Stratus are still missing. If he's working with Renaldo, he may be working with others."

"What's our play?" Alpha asked.

"Good question." Jason sighed and added, "The pieces are moving fast."

"Sir, I have an idea," Smoke interjected.

"What?" Archangel's question snapped back.

"The people in Stratus were isolated from each other, right?"

"Yep," Jewell answered over the persistent typing in the background. "That was the hallmark of the organization. Layers of crappy people that didn't see or know the other crappy people in the organization."

Smoke nodded. "Okay… then why don't

Charley and I assume Camelia and Renaldo's roles here? They come after us and we have him. Positive identification and we can snap the head off Akuma. Which I'm sure Tempest would appreciate." The assassins were supposed to be coming after his friend for killing the Fates, but Tempest had taken measures that would ensure his and his wife's safety. He looked up at Charley.

She put her hand over the phone. "Dahlia and the other man know what I look like and you look just like your brother."

He smiled at her. "Don't underestimate the magic Guardian can perform."

Jason's question drew both of their eyes back to the phone. "Jewell, how much of a social media presence do the couple have?"

"Hold on." There were several long minutes of nothing but typing. "Okay, there are three pictures of Camelia on the Government of Honduras' website, no social media accounts for either Camelia or Renaldo on the big sites. I'll check the lesser-known sites. I'm doing a search of newspaper photos of the couple now."

"In the meantime, where do they live on the island?" Fury asked. "We can start looking at ways to surveil the area."

"According to the information I can find in the Grand Cayman government's computer system, their quarters are being renovated. Oh, hey… yeah, here we go. They live on the Honduran Presidential yacht, named *La Tranquilidad,* which translated means *The Tranquility*. That's a pretty name. Let me do a search of ships registered in Honduras. Oh, wow, look at that. She's a two hundred ninety-three-foot vessel with four levels counting the ship's bridge area."

"Well, Smoke would be at home on the ship," Alpha commented in a smartass kind of way that Smoke actually appreciated after getting his ass handed to him by Archangel for Charley's screw-up, but if he were in her position, he'd probably have done the same thing. No. Definitely, and that is where the rub was, wasn't it?

"Jewell, send me the media exposure on the couple when you have the report. Scrub everything you can think of. If we do this, and I am a long way from agreeing to this strategy, I want to be sure we've sanitized everything."

"Gotcha, will do."

"We are on a hold until we get more intel. Alpha, I need alternatives based on our original discussion. When Smoke gives you the input you need, we'll hash out a way forward or form a hybrid of both of the plans. We have enough assets on that island to start a small war, for God's sake, let's make sure it doesn't come to that. Archangel out."

"I've got my marching orders. Does anyone need anything from me?" Jewell asked and immediately added, "Coolio! CCS out, toodles."

"Smoke, do you need anything from me before the package is delivered?" Alpha asked.

"Negative, sir." Smoke watched as Charley stood and carefully stretched.

"Contact me when you've deciphered that documentation. Alpha out."

"Anubis, give me the line," Fury asked.

"You got it. Annex out."

"So, tell me what in the hell you were thinking."

Smoke looked at Charley and she blinked owlishly. "Can I talk without permission now?"

"Stop the hurt-butt attitude, little girl, and tell me what went through that pea-brain of yours." Fury's sarcasm wet the words until they were soaked in scathing intent.

"She was maybe fourteen and they weren't treating her like it, if you know what I mean. I couldn't just sit there and do nothing."

Fury was silent for a moment before he spoke. "Consider this a learning moment, Charley. Had this mission been more developed or organized and you saw what you saw today in that bar, you would have *had* to let it go. The mission is always the primary objective. The filth of our world is everywhere, but the people we target are the ones hurting hundreds if not thousands. If circumstances were different you wouldn't have been able to help her. Is that something you can live with? I think you need to ask yourself some hard questions and then find a rock-solid answer to land on. This job isn't for everyone, you know that as well as I do. Ask yourself the hard questions, Charley, and then answer them with every ounce of honesty you have. Fury out."

Smoke grabbed the whiskey bottle and took another swig. He kept his eyes on the woman in front of him. The words Fury had laid on her were tough to hear and even tougher to digest. He stood and handed her the bottle. "Have a small drink while I turn the shower on." He strode past her and turned on the hot water. They both needed a bit of TLC thanks to the shit that happened in the tavern. She'd been slapped around tonight, and not just by the bad guys. He ground his teeth together to keep from spewing the swear words he was thinking. He knew what was coming and he probably should have warned her, but a small part... okay, a fucking *huge* part of him wanted her to realize this career wasn't for her. He wanted her to walk away. She wasn't like him or the other people who served Guardian. She hadn't hardened. She hadn't formed that shell that nobody could see through, and he didn't want her to have to go through the process to gain that protection. He'd developed those defenses when he was too damn young. It was surprisingly easy to see that she hadn't.

He reached in and checked the water temperature and grabbed an extra towel from the shelf. He was going to take care of his lover tonight because she was in pain, both physical and mental. He could see it in the way she'd closed in on herself. He checked for soap and shampoo and headed back to take care of his partner and his lover.

CHAPTER 10

Charley stood in the middle of the decrepit little hotel room and stared at the whiskey bottle in her hand. She'd fought so damn hard to get here, to this very moment, to be a full operative in the middle of a Guardian-sanctioned mission, and she'd fucked it up by acting on instinct rather than thinking. Uncorking the whiskey, she took a swig. The liquor hurt the cuts in her mouth, but the warm numbing that would follow would make the pain worth it.

The water turned on in the bathroom. She glanced down at her blood-soaked shirt. Joey's words buzzed through her mind. Ask herself the hard questions? What the hell? The last two-and-a-half years had been nothing but a series of hard questions and harder training. She'd gambled everything on becoming an operative. Everything she used to have or could have in the future could be gone because of the decisions she'd made. Could she make the hard decisions? Fuck, yes.

She closed her eyes and pictured the girl in that dark little tavern. Those perverts kept the girl hidden from most of the establishment, but from where she was sitting, she could see what they were doing, and she could also see that the young one was terrified.

Charley upended the bottle again and downed a larger gulp. There was no decision as far as she was concerned. Helping the people who couldn't help themselves was a pillar of Guardian's foundational tenants. She hadn't endangered the mission, thank God.

Smoke's presence behind her registered as his arms looped around her waist. Thankfully, he didn't pull or tug her back against him. She leaned back and sighed when he took her weight. "Come on. Let me take care of you tonight."

He kissed her temple, and she shook her head before she whispered, "I'm okay."

"Neither one of us is okay right now. We need a shower, some food, and rest." He snaked his hand down her arm and grabbed the whiskey bottle from her. "Warm water. Now."

She turned in his arms and stared up at him. She knew she looked like death warmed over, her nose hurt like a bitch, and if the soreness was any indication, she'd have two wicked black eyes. "I would do what I did over again. Every time."

A gentle smile formed, and his eyes warmed and softened. "I know." He put the whiskey bottle down and took her hand, leading her into the bathroom where he carefully undressed her. His fingers lightly trailed over her bruises before he stripped out of his clothes. They stepped under the hot water. He moved so she was directly under the fall. She tipped her head back and let the deluge rain down her face. Soapy hands grabbed her wrist. Smoke's fingers pressed into the palm and back of her hand and rubbed. The delightful sensation moved as his hands traveled up her arm to her shoulder. He stopped and she opened her eyes. As he lathered his hands again, she took in the sheer masculine beauty standing before her. He was the type of man she hoped she'd marry someday.

Unfortunately, the likelihood of that happening was less than zero. He took her hand in his and started the massage again, avoiding a bruise on her bicep. He carefully spun her around and used those masterful hands to loosen the knots in her shoulders and back. When she knew she couldn't be any more relaxed, he turned her again and sank to his knees in the confined space. He placed her foot on his thigh and... *Oh, damn.*

She swallowed hard and concentrated on the release of tension as he worked her calf muscles. She opened her eyes and stared down at him as he worked the suds across her skin. "Why couldn't you have caved a couple months ago?" The question fell unbidden, but now that she knew the closely guarded secret that had haunted him his entire life, she wanted more. And not just sex—granted, sex with the man was the best she'd ever had, but she longed for more of the unguarded moments where he'd let her help him, more of these times when just being together brought a sense of being whole. She'd thought a sexual relationship with him would be easy, and the physicality of it *was* effortless; the practicality of it was anything but uncomplicated because she'd let herself get attached. Once the man opened himself to her, she tripped and fell straight into a hell of a mess. One of her own making, granted, but becoming emotionally invested in this relationship now, when her freedom would soon be coming to an end, was a mistake.

He set her foot back on the tile and picked up the other one without answering. She closed her eyes and luxuriated in the sensation of his rhythmic massage. When he finished, he lifted and grabbed the shampoo. His eyes traveled over her. She lowered her eyes and dropped her head.

He tucked his finger under her chin and leveraged her eyes back up to him. "Don't hide. Not from me."

"I'm pretty messed up right now." Not just physically, either. Her attraction to him was clouding her short-term goals and wrecking her long-range plans.

He smiled and dropped a kiss on her forehead. "We both are."

"I'm sorry I fucked up and got you yelled at, but I'd do it over again."

He put the shampoo bottle back on the shelf and massaged the foamy suds through her hair.

"I've been yelled at before. So, you've decided to give up being an operative?"

"What?" She jerked and popped her eyes open, hissing as soap ran into her eyes. She spun and washed the shampoo from her hair and face. When she managed to open her eyes and could see again, she turned back to him. "I haven't given up, why would you say that?"

He grabbed the soap and drew it across his chest. Her eyes followed the movement. She grabbed the soap from him and took over washing his rock-hard abs. "You haven't answered me."

He turned around when she put gentle pressure on his hip. She started at his shoulders and rubbed his back in circles. "If you would do the same thing again and compromise a mission, you'd be removed."

"I don't think so. Guardian protects those who can't protect themselves. It is their core belief." She knew that deep in her soul.

"And if by saving one small girl you inadvertently ruin a case being built against a person who ran, say, a sex slave ring, you'd have hurt how many other children?"

Her hands paused on his back as she listened to his question. "That wasn't the case this time."

"No, it wasn't. This time it was a group of assassins who we know nothing about. We were sent to gather intel so we could identify and apprehend——"

"Or kill," she interjected, and Smoke tensed before he nodded. She felt it more than saw it as she moved her soapy hands over his lower back.

"Or eliminate. But had you been under observation, how hard would it have been to slip a knife into a fistfight? You and I both know it takes one thrust in the right area and you're dead. Or for that matter, a needle full of poison, a gun with a suppressor..." He stopped speaking. Her hand on his back rose and fell with the quick breaths of his lungs. She blinked as she watched the lift and fall. He was upset, but his voice didn't convey anger, it was almost as if he felt—

He spoke again, "And if you were being followed, they would have identified me. Whether or not you choose to admit it to yourself, your actions today put us both in jeopardy. You can't take a chance like that again."

She swirled the soap on his back a couple more times before she stepped aside and let the shower wash the suds away. "I can't promise you I won't, but I do promise not to put you in jeopardy."

He reached over for the shampoo without turning around to face her. After he put the bottle back, he spoke. "I don't think you understand, Charley. I don't give a flying fuck about me. I'm old and on my way out of this game. You have too much life to live to be that careless. That's why Fury was so mad and that's why I'm... upset."

She stepped past him so she could see his face. "What do you mean you're on your way out?"

He tipped his head back and rinsed the shampoo from his hair. He turned off the shower and pushed the curtain open, grabbing a towel for her and one for him. She quickly toweled off and wrapped her hair in the terrycloth.

Smoke wrapped the towel around him and padded out into the bedroom. She grabbed another towel and wrapped it around her, following him out. Smoke grabbed the bottle and took a slug before he nodded toward the small fridge. "Hungry?"

"No. You can't ignore my question."

He snorted and tipped the bottle again. "Oh, hell yes, I can."

She grabbed the bottle from him. "Okay, let me rephrase that: you damn well better not ignore my question." She lifted the bottle a little too quickly and winced when her ribs complained.

"Or what?" With two steps, he was in front of the fridge. He pulled out a loaf of bread, sandwich meat, cheese, and mayo.

"Perfect, more sandwiches." She rolled her eyes. She used to like them, but it was about all Smoke knew how to make, which made sense now. Reading food labels had to be a bitch for him. She took another drink and sat on the bed. "Why did you say that? That you were on your way out?"

He stood and started making a sandwich. She watched as the muscles in his back moved under his tanned skin. "I'm getting old, Charley. Old and this profession don't do well together unless you are in a support role. I can never sit behind a desk like Bengal or Anubis. I'd be shit as an instructor. So, that limits my ability to stay with Guardian after my usefulness is past. Maybe I'll find a new boat and one day just drift away, leaving all this behind me." He lifted his hands and motioned to the shitty little room where they were waiting for direction.

She lifted the bottle again and took a small swig. "There are things you could do."

His laugh was bitter and sharp. "Yeah? Like

what? Run a charter service for people who do what I did but only better? Or how about being left out of operations because I'm over the hill and can't contribute? No, thanks. I've had a taste of what that feels like. I can assure you I don't want to go back to being a glorified babysitter. It sucks worse than being put on a shelf as a relic."

She sat the bottle on her thigh and held it in a death grip as she tried to calm herself. Purposely, she counted to one hundred—in three different languages—while he made short work of the sandwich he'd made. Finally, she moved the bottle to the nightstand just in case she felt like using it as a club over his block head.

He glanced at her as she stood. "About that babysitting gig, sorry it inconvenienced you." She headed into the bathroom.

"Aww fuck, Charley..." he called after her.

"Like he could say something now that would make me any less angry," she mumbled to herself as she collected her jeans, panties, and bra. The shirt was a horror, but she turned it inside out and put it on before she found her socks and put on her shoes. A pat to her back pocket of her jeans assured her she still had the bank card issued to her... yeah, it was only this morning. Man, the shit that could be packed into fifteen hours was unbelievable. Smoke stood as she walked out. "Where in the hell do you think you're going?"

"To get something other than a fucking sandwich to eat and to give myself space so I don't say or do anything that I'll regret."

"Let me get my clothes on and I'll come with you."

"Don't bother, space requires you not being there."

"Damn it, Charley, we're partners! Give me two minutes."

She spun and glared at him. "Are we? Really? I think the answer to that is no. You drew the short straw and were saddled as my babysitter, remember? Well, I'm an adult, in case you missed that the last time we *fucked,* and guess what? You're fired."

She wrenched the door open and stalked out into the darkness. "Charley, damn it!"

She spun on her heel and flew two middle fingers in his direction before she spun again and walked away.

The entire organization wanted her to fold her cards and walk away. She'd gotten that vibe from Archangel and all the way down the line. Damn it! She kicked a rock and hissed as her ribs screamed at her. Fuck. She'd worked so damn hard to be treated as an equal. She'd trained harder, taken more tests, and passed with higher standards than anyone else. Her family had made the path nearly impossible and she'd fought every roadblock only to come to this point. She was a burden. Fucking fabulous.

CHAPTER 11

The greasy cheeseburger and fries sat cold on her plate while she stared out the window of the small mom-and-pop restaurant that she'd finally found after walking through a nearly deserted Georgetown for about an hour. When the cruise ships weren't in port, the traffic, both pedestrian and vehicular, slowed as did the rhythm of the city. The bell over the door jangled, drawing her attention away from the cars that passed on the street.

A tall man entered the establishment and every nerve in her body tensed. He was the type of man women would drool over. His dark auburn hair flopped in front of his eyes. He made no pretense about where he was heading. She gripped the steak knife she'd placed beside her when she realized she'd managed to lose her weapon at the tavern along with a fuckton of cash. Whoever picked up her purse was living large right about now. They hadn't questioned her about the money or the weapon at the holding cell, so both were probably stolen from the booth where she'd been sitting.

He slid into the booth across from her. "You are a hard woman to find."

She lifted an eyebrow and waited. He leaned back and pushed the hair out of his face. His eyes, a golden topaz color with dark rings around the outside, seemed almost like colored lenses.

"Smoke is going crazy."

She snorted and released her death grip on the handle of the steak knife to a more comfortable hold. "Why?"

"Guess he thinks you can't take care of yourself. That knife you got in your hand won't deter many people." He reached across the table and slid her plate toward him.

"It would kill at least one." She watched as he added ketchup to the burger and salted the fries. "Hungry?"

He glanced up and shrugged. "Been a day or

two since I ate and it's obvious you're not going to eat the food you ordered."

"What's your name?"

He took a bite of the burger and chewed it as he stared at her. Finally, swallowing his food, he picked up a fry. "I have a lot of them."

Fair enough, they all did. "Okay, what do I call you? Besides, you know, a cheeseburger stealing asshole?"

He smiled as he popped the fry into his mouth. "Reaper said you were a live wire."

"Reaper is a dick at times."

"You don't know him very well. He's actually a dick all the time." The man lifted his finger for the waitress and ordered two sodas, one for him and one for her. "You can call me Phoenix."

"I'd say nice to meet you, but I'm assuming you already called my babysitter and told him you've found me." She stopped talking as the waitress reappeared with two sodas. After the server left, Charley turned her attention back to Phoenix.

"Babysitter? Thought you were his partner."

"That what he told you?"

The man's brow creased. "No. An assumption on my part."

"Huh. Mine, too."

The guy paused with her burger halfway to his mouth. "Care to elaborate?" He took another huge bite.

She sighed and looked out the window again, keeping his reflection in her view as she stared down the road. She shook her head. "Nope. Wouldn't do any good."

She watched as Reaper walked out of the darkness on the other side of the street. He advanced with that damn stalking prowl. He entered the cafe and slid into the booth next to Phoenix, who moved over, making room for the assassin. Reaper glanced at the half-eaten plate of food and nodded. "Good, about damn time."

Phoenix shrugged and took another bite. Reaper glanced over at her and raised his hand for the waitress. When she arrived, he ordered a large salad, a fruit plate, and another cheeseburger.

"Hungry?" Charley asked when the waitress left.

"Not really. The salad and fruit are for him." He nodded to Phoenix, who was done with the burger and was working on the fries.

"Why are you here?" She took a drink of her soda and watched the redhead devour the fries.

"Because you are." Reaper shrugged as if the

short answer revealed the obvious reason for two of Guardian's assets to trail her.

She pulled out her bank card and waved it at the waitress. Reaper sighed, "Man, don't leave. If you do, he may stop eating, and God only knows when he'll be able to eat again."

She looked from Reaper to Phoenix, who seemed to have zoned out and was one with his fries. The waitress came with the salad and fruit which Phoenix promptly started to obliterate. She handed the card to the waitress. "For everything."

The woman nodded, dropped it in her pocket, and stopped at a table of new customers that had entered after Reaper. She caught Reaper's eye and lifted an eyebrow in question.

Phoenix muttered in between shoveling fries into his mouth, "Just tell her."

"His work leaves a certain odor. One he can sense and taste for days, sometimes longer. Eating isn't always possible."

"Were you here on a mission?" She glanced at Phoenix, who shook his head.

"No, but the last time out was pretty intense." Phoenix shoved a forkful of salad in his mouth and chomped away.

The door opened again, and Smoke strode

through. He slid into the booth next to her, forcing her over as he slid. She glared at him and he narrowed his eyes. Just as he opened his mouth to speak, Reaper talked over him.

"If you're going to have a domestic situation, I suggest you go back to the room. We are far too public for anything either of you need to say to each other."

She turned to look at the assassin across from her. "I don't need your advice or tutelage. Thank you."

Reaper snorted and shook his head. "Little one, you need a hell of a lot of seasoning and thicker skin if you're going to make it in this world."

She leaned over the table and hissed, "How would you know?"

"We all know," Smoke answered for Reaper. "If you were more seasoned or had thicker skin, an offhand comment about babysitting wouldn't have sent you off the deep end."

She leaned back and shook her head. "It wasn't just that."

Smoke shrugged. "We've all had our asses handed to us. You think you're the only one who Archangel has taken a piece out of? Put yourself in his shoes for a minute and you'd realize he is responsible for every one of us. Our successes *and* our fuck ups. The reputation of the organization and its integrity is on him to guard."

She rolled her shoulders. Unless she told them about her past, her family involvement, there was no way they'd understand, but they were right. She needed thicker skin.

"Would you like to order? I'll get you a menu." The waitress spoke to Smoke as she set Reaper's cheeseburger down and fished Charley's bank card and signature slip from her apron pocket.

Smoke glanced up at the special boards and shook his head. "No, thank you."

Charley stopped the waitress. "Ma'am, he's just being polite. If I know him, he's starving. Would you bring him your fried chicken special and a glass of water, please?"

"Sure. You know, you look a lot like that actor."

Charley laughed. "He gets that all the time. Would he be hanging out with us, eating fried chicken if he was Chris Collins?"

The waitress laughed. Reaper chuckled, "Yeah, I heard that guy was a vegetarian, and the latest article I read said he was in Nepal filming the next installment of that trilogy, what was the name?"

Phoenix spoke around a mouthful of salad, "*Infinite Horizons.*"

"Right," Reaper agreed.

The waitress gave Smoke another look and nodded, confused enough to agree. "I'll get that chicken out to you."

Smoke bumped her knee in appreciation.

Phoenix spoke as Smoke's knee rested against hers. "You really have two pretty good shiners, you know." Phoenix pointed at his own eyes with his finger. "But it doesn't look bad, the bone doesn't look dented or bent." He moved side to side to see her nose from different angles. "The swelling isn't as bad as it would be with a break."

"You speak from experience?" She smiled at him when she asked.

He nodded. "Four breaks." He pointed to his nose. "Reset it myself three times."

"Reset it?" Charley shivered. "Not my idea of self-aid."

Phoenix laughed. "It is if you want to breathe."

Charley leaned into Smoke as the conversation switched to other topics. She'd overreacted, and instead of making her feel like a moron, these men, these hardcore killers, had taken the time to make her feel included and supported. For the first time since she'd begun with Guardian, she felt like she belonged. Not with management, but she wasn't supposed to, was she? Her objective at the beginning of this journey was to understand as much as she could. What she'd found wasn't what she'd expected. The instant inclusion she'd anticipated based on what she'd seen from the outside looking in hadn't happened. But the support these men provided her, even after telling her she needed to grow in the career, was the crux of what she'd been looking for. The sense of belonging.

Smoke's chicken came out and Phoenix helped himself to a wing and a thigh before Smoke defended his plate with Charley's steak knife. She laughed until her sides hurt which, because of the bruised ribs, didn't take much. After she paid for Smoke's food, they all meandered out of the small cafe.

"I'll be around tomorrow morning. Sierra Team and your package arrived early. They're sitting on the bogies until we get back. Then they'll rack out. When they take over, I'll bring your shit." Reaper grabbed the back of Phoenix's neck. "I'm going to get this guy a gallon of ice cream and then we'll head back."

Phoenix moved only his eyes to look at Reaper.

The tawny gold orbs narrowed. Reaper smiled. "Fine, two gallons, but I get a bowlful."

"Deal." Phoenix spun out of Reaper's hold and lifted a hand. "Whatever it takes, Bambi."

"Charley," she corrected him.

"Nah, you look like a Bambi."

Smoke chuckled and winked at her.

"Fine, but you tell anyone else that I'm answering to that, and we're going to go a few rounds, and I won't stop… for as long as it takes."

"I'll let you heal up a bit before I take you up on that." Phoenix waved and fell into step with Reaper, who whistled a slow tune as they walked away.

"They're pretty amazing men." Charley glanced up at Smoke. "And so are you. I'm sorry I stormed out. I hit my limit and I needed to get away."

Smoke dropped his arm over her shoulder and turned her back toward the crappy little hotel. "Another thing we'll work on."

"Thank you."

"For what? Being a fantastic partner? Introducing you to two men who will have your back for the rest of your natural life or making an ass of myself because I selfishly wanted you to quit?"

She stopped and looked up at him. "Why?"

He wrapped her in his arms and pulled her against him. "Because you've become special to me, Charley. Only one other person in my life has affected me this deeply."

"Sage."

He nodded. "He's an amazing man."

"So are you." She toed up and kissed him. "You don't give yourself enough credit in that department."

He broke the embrace and they walked in silence for a while. "You know, you're important to me, too."

"Why?" His quiet question weighed heavy between them.

She gave the question the consideration it deserved before she responded. "At first, it was just a sexual attraction." She laughed and stopped short when her ribs reminded her to behave. "Then, for four months, you taught me things I'd never believe I'd be able to know or master. I can talk to you. There are very few people in my life I'm myself with, who I trust enough to be myself. You're one."

"Who else?" he asked as they crossed a street.

"Mom. She's wonderful. Up to a point, my father. I guess you'd call him intense, and he *is* stuck in his ways, which isn't bad, but it is damn formidable. Besides them, I trust Joey, Jacob, Jace, and Jewell. Jade, too. She was my self-defense instructor and that gave me confidence." There were a few more, but that information—like all the rest of her past—wasn't hers to share.

"So, I'm a friend." He nodded to himself.

She nodded. "And my lover and my partner. All put together, you're the most important person in my universe right now."

He stopped her again and stared down at her. "Yes. That."

She smiled up at him. "That." The depth of emotion in his eyes took her breath away. She placed her hand on his chest over his heart.

He covered her hand. "And this."

She looked up at him and nodded. "This, too." She licked her lips and whispered. "Be careful."

He nodded. "Always." He dropped a soft kiss against her lips and broke away. He took her hand and they turned and walked the remaining distance to the hotel in silence. Smoke opened the door and she entered. He didn't turn on the light and she didn't need it. By an unspoken mutual agreement, they undressed without a word. She took his hand and led him to the bed.

He pulled her into his side and covered them with the sheet and comforter. She hissed and winced several times as she settled on the mattress. “I'm sorry I can't make love tonight.” Her eyes popped open. Fuck or sex, damn it, she really needed to stop dropping that 'L' word.

“I don't need to make love until you're better. I just want to hold you.” Smoke turned to his side and kissed her temple. “Go to sleep, Charley, tomorrow will be here soon enough.”

She settled in against him and closed her eyes. She hurt just about everywhere, but it didn't matter. The one place she didn't feel pain was deep inside her. There she felt connected, a part of something larger and even closer to Smoke. She pushed away the niggling thought of what was looming on the horizon. She'd soak in the feeling of contentment and belonging so she could remember it when this part of her life was ripped away.

CHAPTER 12

Smoke answered the door wearing only his jeans when Reaper knocked the next morning. Charley was soaking in a warm shower to loosen her sore muscles. His headache had diminished to a dull thud, and the coffee Reaper held in his hands was the remedy he needed for what remained.

"Take this, I'll grab the kits from Alpha." Reaper handed him a tray with four coffees and two bags of something that smelled like cinnamon and butter. He opened one bag after he set the tray down and said a small thank you for the unexpected gift. Reaper kicked open the door that had started to close and dumped two huge duffle bags on the floor. He held out his hand.

Smoke narrowed his eyes. "You want a tip or something?"

"No, asshole, I want my coffee. You're standing in front of it."

"Oh." He moved to the side and opened the first bag. Clothes on top. Men's clothing, so this was his bag. He unzipped the other and grabbed clean clothes for Charley and took them into the bathroom. "Reaper's here. Phoenix won't be too far behind. Clean clothes are on the counter." He pulled the curtain back and tried hard not to wince at the bruises under her eyes.

She opened her eyes. "I'll be out soon."

"Good, Reaper brought coffee and cinnamon rolls."

"Holy shit. I'm coming." She turned off the water. He laughed and left the bathroom to let her get ready. Phoenix was sitting in the only chair, his back to the corner and eyes on the door. Reaper had taken up space on the floor leaning against the wall. They both had a huge, frosted roll and a cup of coffee.

Smoke grabbed one of the two pastries left in the white bag and a cup of coffee. He planted his ass on his side of the bed. "Any movement from our bogies last night?" He took a sizable hunk out of the roll and groaned at the deliciousness.

Phoenix shook his head while he was finishing the food in his mouth. "Not until early this morning."

"That's how I got the rolls and coffee." Reaper saluted him with his cup. "Followed the man and woman to a small bakery. I entered after them, but the woman took forever to decide she wanted a no-taste latte, so I ordered for us and then fixed my coffee while they ordered and then left."

"The man and woman who I made contact with yesterday?" Charley came out of the bathroom. Her hair was wet, but she looked better in clean clothes and after a night's rest.

Phoenix closed one eye and cocked his head. "Hell of a pair of shiners you got going on there, Bambi."

"Seriously, my name isn't Bambi. You caught that, right?"

Phoenix shook his head. "Yeah, but I think of a tuna fish when I hear that other name. You are not a tuna." He shrugged and took a huge bite of his roll.

She snorted dismissively and made her way to

the coffee. Taking the top off, she inhaled the aroma and sighed. "Well, at least I can still smell."

"Told you, I don't think it's broken. Just abused." Phoenix stopped with his food halfway to his mouth and suddenly put the thing down. He pushed it toward Reaper, who pulled it away from the assassin and moved it to the other side of him, out of Phoenix's eyesight. Smoke opened the drawer to the nightside table and sat his half-eaten breakfast on the wax paper it was wrapped in out of view. Phoenix's memories fucked up his ability to eat and he could certainly understand. What he did was second only to Tempest in the macabre and disgusting category. Tempest made statements. Phoenix made torches. His specific way of removing monsters was rarely used, but when it was called into play, Phoenix paid the physical and mental price for months afterward.

Charley watched the food disappear from sight and put two and two together. She took the white paper bag and set it on the other side of the television before she moved over to sit beside him. After taking a drink of her coffee, she asked again, "The man and woman, did you notice anything weird about—"

Reaper's phone rang. He swiped the face and

put it on speaker. "Sunset Operative Fourteen, stand by."

Reaper rolled his eyes. "I should have been Operative Thirteen."

Charley looked from one man to the next. "Why?"

"That was my number. Football, Basketball, Baseball, Lacrosse." Reaper shrugged. "I told her, too."

"Like she'd give it up to you," Phoenix snorted.

"And here I thought she was giving it up to you on the regular," Fury snipped.

Charley, who had just taken a drink of coffee, gasped and choked at the comment. Smoke grabbed her coffee so she could hold her ribs as she coughed. Damn, that looked painful as fuck.

"That was over before it began," Reaper growled back at Fury.

"Smart woman," Fury countered.

"CCS on. Who's dying?"

"Charley," Smoke and Reaper said in unison.

"Bambi," Phoenix said afterward. That earned him a glare from Charley. She carefully took several shallow breaths before sitting up straighter.

"Okay, one, Bambi... that is the cutest code-name ever, and two, are you okay?"

"Just peachy, and it is not my codename."

"It should be," Jewell retorted.

"I agree," Fury added his two cents.

"What are we agreeing on? Annex on," Anubis asked.

"Bambi should be Charley's codename," Jewell answered before Charley could speak.

"Bambi. Fierce. Alpha online," Jacob chuckled and that earned Phoenix a pointed finger and a glare from Charley.

"Archangel on. I like it. Make it happen."

"What? No!" Charley stared at the phone.

"Done." Anubis' comment dripped in humor.

"Fuck me."

Reaper pointed at Smoke. "His territory, not ours."

Phoenix nodded. "True."

Charley closed her eyes and muttered obscenities under her breath.

"Now that we've established a new codename and someone has staked claim to shit I never want to hear about again, give me an update on what's going on. The Annex is up first." Archangel took control of the meeting.

"Roger that, sir. CCS scraped data and we've determined based on the information Jewell's people have provided that taking over the identities of Camelia and Renaldo isn't a sustainable plan. First is the physical differences between the Uribeses and our assets, the second is the number of photographs available from sources other than social media. While the Uribeses aren't splashy, they have been photographed with heads of state and at numerous charitable events."

"What are our options then?" Archangel asked.

"My vote is for Smoke and Charley to wire that boat and blow everyone to hell when the meeting takes place. Let Satan figure out who's who," Fury's voice grated over the connection.

"And that is why you are not in charge of the operation," Alpha laughed.

Fury grunted, "It would solve our problem."

"Only if Clayborne shows. He could send his minions," Anubis countered.

"Enough. Options. Now," Archangel snapped.

Anubis answered, "We've got a two-pronged plan of action. First, Reaper and Phoenix will set up listening tech that is being flown down as we speak. We've rented a ship berthed on the opposite side of the harbor, but it will give you a straight line of sight to the ship. The tech is sensitive enough to capture anything that is said. Line it up and configure it to send to CCS. They'll be monitoring it twenty-four seven. When you've finished that, call me and we'll discuss why Phoenix is there instead of here."

All eyes traveled to the assassin sitting in the corner. Phoenix closed his eyes and dropped his head back against the wall.

"I'm sorry, I failed to hear your acknowledgement." Anubis' reprimand came across loud and clear.

"Roger, we copy all, sir," Reaper replied.

"What's the second prong?" Archangel prompted.

"Oh, that's mine," Alpha spoke. "My wife is a wiz with satellite imagery, and she's found an area we believe the submarine that brought Clayborne and his cabal is... parked? Do you park a sub?"

Smoke snorted. "Normally they are docked like a ship."

"Yeah, but that's just it. In the imagery we've gone through, it shows a subtle difference in the reef area where we believe the bogies came onto the island. Camouflage netting is our bet."

"So, they disembarked and someone stayed on the sub and has it sitting at the bottom of the ocean, just off the island." Charley looked at Smoke. "Could we somehow take the sub?"

"To what end?" He wasn't following her thinking.

"To be on it if Clayborne goes back to it and to ensure he doesn't get away," Alpha answered. "That is another option, but the one we've devised is bent differently. If we take out the sub, disable it, we have him landlocked."

"It's an island that isn't far away from any other island. He can steal a boat and be off it before we know he's gone. Hell, we wouldn't know he was gone because we don't know what he looks like now."

"I'd really like to know what he looks like then," Smoke said out loud when he probably should have kept his mouth shut.

"Why?" Jewell asked.

"Well, consider this. What if Clayborne left Korea by other means—the sub for example—and had someone else transporting his watch. You'd think he'd changed his appearance, right?"

Dead silence met his musing. He glanced at Charley, who was smiling at him. She leaned over and whispered, "You're fucking brilliant."

His chest filled with pride because she thought

he was smart. Those words had rarely been uttered in his presence and never in conjunction with him. At least not until Demos had pulled him from the shithole of a life he'd been living in.

"It is possible. The type of sub we believe he's using is one of the older Sang-O versions. That class of sub is about a hundred feet long and four-teen feet wide. She can travel at a speed of 9 knots and has a range of fifteen hundred nautical miles."

Smoke leaned forward. "Alpha, is that sub capable of being armed?"

"Yes. Two tubes."

"Sir, the Uribeses live on a floating target." Smoke glanced around the room. "If Clayborne is going to make a statement..."

"He'll blow the boat out of the water," Fury finished for him.

Anubis voiced an objection. "But Clayborne is looking to expand, not diminish his business. Remember, Renaldo is believed to be one of the higher members of Three's organization. If he takes out Renaldo, what is his intro to the upper levels of Stratus?"

"Good point. At this point, we don't know. Smoke, you and Charley disable that thing. Take it out of commission but don't shred it. I'm sure the tech is old, and the damn thing is probably a rust bucket, but the DoD will want to put it under a microscope."

"It isn't technically in international waters," Alpha threw in a stumbling block.

"It will be by the time the Navy boards her," Archangel chuckled. "Smoke, you make sure the damn thing can be towed from where you disable her."

"Roger that, sir, but in order to do that, Charley and I are going to have to make a few dives to rescue some of my equipment that has settled to the bottom of the Caribbean." He needed angled blasting caps that he'd manufactured, plus they'd need to cut the C-4 and portion it based on the mission. "We'll need the specs of the sub." He looked at her and she nodded. It would be a team effort.

Alpha answered, "On its way with the tech for listening to Camelia and Renaldo. Sierra Team is still monitoring the bogie phones and they've split into two teams so they have twenty-four-hour coverage."

"Jewell, get a picture of Clayborne sent to Reaper and the new phones that Smoke and Charley have in Alpha's care package. Smoke, keep

Anubis advised on the dives and your status, let us know when you'll be disabling the sub. Reaper and Phoenix, you have Camelia and Renaldo. We need to identify Clayborne and we need to do it ASAP. From the profile we've built on Renaldo, he isn't stupid on the regular, so he's not going to meet Akuma where he doesn't have the advantage. He has leverage on the boat because he has security there as a foreign diplomat. I want this wrapped. The more we dick around with this bastard, the more exposed we become. Jewell, I want pictures of these bogies we've been following run against every known database. We have to identify Clayborne before he leverages another alliance. Although, thankfully, Renaldo has delayed that event, I don't think he's obliterated his opportunity. We have work to do, ladies and gentlemen, get to it. Archangel out."

"Alpha out."

"CCS out."

"Annex out."

"Well, that was fun," Fury drawled. "I'm here if you need me. Don't need me. Rose out."

CHAPTER 13

"Fury's so sweet, bless his heart, y'all." Charley blinked innocently before she rolled her eyes.

"Your phones are somewhere in those duffle bags, my phone is already blowing up." Reaper glanced at Phoenix. "I didn't tell them shit."

"They heard me on the phone. It doesn't matter." Phoenix lifted out of the chair and extended his hand to Reaper to help him up. "We'd better go figure out how to be techie types. You two be careful. If you need anything throw us a text."

"We will. You two be careful, too. Whatever it takes."

"For as long as it takes, and let's hope for

Archangel's sanity it doesn't take long," Reaper chuckled as he followed Phoenix out of the room.

"Time to see what Alpha decided we homeless people needed." Smoke rubbed his hands together and unzipped the industrial-sized duffle.

Charley snorted and headed for the white paper bag. "After I eat." She sat on the floor with her coffee and pastry, munching away as he unloaded the bag. A wallet with identification, passport with the same name on it. Not his, of course. A wad of money, credit cards in the same name as the identification, and a new telephone were wrapped together. The next bundle revealed a forty-five, shoulder and ankle holsters, ammo, and a 911 Interceptor which was a wicked-as-fuck blade. Then there were clothes, shoes, toiletries, and a small digital recorder. There were three mini-disks in a case taped to the back. At the bottom of the bag were a wetsuit, snorkel, mask, and dive fins. They'd need air tanks, but if needed they could retrieve the ones they abandoned or better yet purchase new tanks in case the spot where they'd dumped theirs was being monitored or the area had been rigged. No, retrieving the old equipment wasn't worth the chance of being seen.

He started to put most of the equipment back into the bag. "Are you ready to dive today?"

Charley glanced up at him examining his passport. "Do I want to? No. Can I? Yes. I don't think my nose is broken, so the mask will be uncomfortable but not a showstopper. My ribs are what will hold me back. I'm sore, not going to lie. If we need to use brute strength underwater, I'll be useless."

"Once we find the old girl, I should be able to salvage some tools to help us. Plus, there is this." He pulled out a small package that was double-wrapped. He opened it and lifted out an array of blasting caps, pins, det cord, and C-4.

Charley chuckled. "Well, well, it looks like Alpha knows how to throw a party."

"Indeed. If need be, we'll use this to manipulate the surroundings so we can access the equipment we need. Using it on the actual safes would be—"

"An epic cluster." Charley used her hands and puffed out her cheeks, making an explosion noise.

"Correct. Let me grab a shower while you go through your bag and we'll head out." He leaned across the bag and kissed her tenderly.

"Thank you for last night."

His brow furrowed. "For what? We went to sleep."

She laughed and leaned forward, placing her forehead on his shoulder. "No, for coming after me and talking to me. This sense of belonging, of fitting in… well, it's something I've worked damn hard to achieve. I think I fit in with you and with Reaper and Phoenix."

He smiled. "Aww, Bambi, of course, you fit in."

"Asshole," she snorted and held her ribs lightly.

"Yeah, but I'm your asshole. You're stuck with me."

"For a while, yeah." Her eyes darkened and she glanced away from him.

"I'll gamble that the time we have left is going to be the best either of us has ever spent."

She shook her head and sighed, "I'm not a good bet."

He moved the bag so he could sit beside her. "It's a damn good thing I'm not gambling, then."

She leaned into him. "You don't know what I'm trying to do here or what's going to happen."

"Because you won't tell me. I don't think you trust me yet. I'll wait. When you do, I'll be here to support you. You've got a heart the size of this island. I don't want to see that diminish, and I'm afraid this profession will do just that."

Charley sat up and stared into his eyes. "Yes,

this profession will. But this isn't the end of the line for me."

Smoke held her gaze. She was trying to tell him something without using words that would compromise what she felt she couldn't say. He pushed a strand of damp hair back behind her ear. "I'll ride the train with you and help you any way I can. The moment you want me to leave, you say so and I'll unhook."

She leaned against him. "It isn't going to be a smooth ride."

"Thank goodness. We'd both be bored to tears."

She leaned up awkwardly and kissed him. "Well, hang onto your board shorts because I have a feeling shit's about to get real."

CHAPTER 14

Charley sat down in the water and removed her fins. She'd been almost useless down there, but Smoke had been amazing. He was able to open one safe without any issue. They loaded the net bags they had with everything they could shove into them. She ferried them to the beach and tugged them as far as she could before she secured the line to a tree and dove back down to watch him as he used a small charge to dislodge the other safe from a sandbar and muscle the thing over so he could open it. The buoyancy of the water helped, but undoubtedly it was the man's brute force that ensured he had been able to open it. She watched him work and kept her eyes peeled for any uninvited guests. Except for a random barracuda and two lazy nurse sharks, they were uninterrupted.

Smoke came back into the water and took her fins, helping her to stand up. Her ribs were screaming like a banshee on Halloween, but she wasn't going to let her injuries sideline her any more than they had. Taking off the mask wasn't as painful as putting it on and making sure it was sealed. Together, they moved up to the assortment of supplies they'd retrieved and made several trips to the vehicle they'd picked up from Sierra Team. A rental from the airport, it was big enough to lock away the supplies in the trunk.

When they were almost done, she unzipped her wetsuit and pulled out a small silver frame. "I saw this and thought it might mean something to you." The picture was damaged by water, but she could still see Smoke and another man, who she believed to be Sage, laughing and smiling.

He took the frame and smiled down at the photo. "That's us on our first mission together. Cuba. I was on loan to Homeland Security. He was shot a couple days after this photo was taken."

"In Cuba?"

He nodded. "Yeah, dirty bomb manufacturing which was protected by the Cuban government."

He smiled and tapped the frame. "It means a lot that you'd think to pick this up." He handed it back to her and picked up her tanks and his.

She grabbed the masks, snorkels, and fins and followed him to the rental. "You haven't had many people do nice things for you, have you?"

He carefully set the tanks on a towel on the back seat, and she put the other equipment on the floorboard where the mat would protect the vehicle from any seawater that remained. They got into the car after stripping out of their wetsuits and placing them in a waterproof bag to be rinsed out. He threw a shirt on over his board shorts and she slipped into a pair of shorts and a t-shirt before they headed back to the shitty little hotel. It didn't escape her that he hadn't replied.

Finally, as they pulled onto Sea View Road, he answered her, "As an adult, I have. Not as a child. Guardian's shrinks tell me that's fucked me up."

Charley nodded and put on one of the two ten-dollar pair of aviator sunglasses she'd picked up this morning. Smoke was wearing the other pair along with a ball cap she'd found to replace the one he'd lost in the bar fight. "We're all fucked up one way or another. Although, personally, I can't blame it on my upbringing. My folks were strict, loving, and totally normal."

"Yeah? Then what fucked you up?"

Charley lowered her eyes to her hands and started to pick at her nails. "Remember how I told you I was prone to get into trouble?"

"I seem to recall something about that."

"I was in Europe right after high school graduation. I gave the slip to my friends and chaperones and wandered around in Italy because hey, in my estimation, at fourteen I was a grown-ass woman and I could do what I wanted, right?"

"You graduated high school at fourteen?" He glanced over at her.

"Homeschooled, remember? Nothing else to do except study, so I put my mind to it and graduated early. I figured it would be a way to escape the corral my parents had built around me." She leaned back in the seat and stuck her arm out the open window, letting the wind buffet against her hand.

"You were telling me about Italy."

"Right. Rome, actually. Anyway, big, badass me." She closed her eyes for a moment and then turned in her seat to look at him. "Did you know that the Russian Mafia deals heavily in human trafficking?"

He sent her a glance and nodded.

"Yeah, well, I found out. Firsthand. I was taken and drugged and... indoctrinated." It was the easiest way to say it, to vocalize what horrors had transpired in those drug-hued nightmares.

The car swerved and skidded to a stop on the gravel beside the road. Smoke grabbed the wheel and twisted his grip around the metal. "How long did they have you?"

"Three days, or so I was told. I was so far out of it I don't remember much." Except for every time they came for her. Her voice broke as she spoke, but she cleared her throat and pushed past the pain. "My dad, he ahhh... hired some people... They found me and a few others."

"And that is why you want to be an operative?"

"No, that is why I want to head an organization that can and will exterminate the evil that is in this world."

"Setting your sights high, aren't you?" He reached out and laid his hand over hers.

She glanced up at him. "I'm known for aiming at impossible targets, but if you don't try..."

"You'll always wonder what if."

She nodded. "Exactly. So, being fucked up is something we have in common."

"I wish it weren't. In the group home, some of the girls who couldn't consent didn't have a choice. But I knew who took their choice away. I made them pay."

"I didn't have that satisfaction, but I will. Someday, I will." She squeezed his hand. "My motivation aside, you have to understand that dreams that big won't come easy. If you want to unhitch now, I won't blame you."

Smoke leaned back, still holding her hand. "I've had two partners in my life and that is only because of a change of policy at Guardian. Both of you mean the world to me. I will always carry Sage in my heart as a brother I chose."

She looked up at him; her reflection in his mirrored aviators looked back at her. "And me?"

He glanced down to where their hands joined. "I'll carry you in my heart, too, but for an entirely different reason. One that has nothing to do with the feelings for a brother or a sister."

She tugged at his hand, making him look up. Her heart pounded and her mouth dried as she struggled to ask the next question. "How?"

He lifted her hand and placed her palm against

his. His hand dwarfed hers, but he held it gently. "How do I feel about you?"

She nodded, unable to speak and not daring to breathe.

"I don't really know. Is it love?" He smiled and lifted her hand, kissing the back of it. "I'm terrified to say yes."

"Why?" Her one-word questions were like needles under her skin, erupting because they were so sharp that nothing could stop them from being asked.

"You. You're still quicksilver."

She batted the word around in her brain and came up with nothing. "I don't understand."

"You're still young, Charley. You're changing, growing, moving, becoming. You flow like mercury, and I'm at a point in my life where I don't want the craziness that comes from the uncertainty of that process. So, yeah, I'm terrified to admit that I'm falling in love with you." He sighed heavily, and she did the only thing she could.

She smacked him in the arm with her free hand.

"What the actual fuck?" He dropped her hand and rubbed his bicep before he pointed at her. "That shit is getting old."

"Then stop assuming you know what's going on with me because it's pretty damn obvious you don't. I just got done telling you what happened to me. Do you think for an iota that those fuckers didn't change me? That I didn't grow up in that instant? That I haven't been laser-focused to reach my goal since the minute I realized what I needed to do? Quicksilver? Oh, God, no, I'm on a single course that I plotted a long, long time ago. I'm not changing. I haven't changed my focus in eight years, and I know exactly what I want, and I've worked damn hard to get where I am. I want you, damn it. Somewhere in the last four months, my words about hooking up have become a fucking smokescreen for wanting more from you but not being able to admit it."

He pulled his glasses off and reached for hers. She let him take them off. He leaned forward and kissed her; the gentleness of the contact damn near brought tears to her eyes. She could feel him smile when a full-body shiver raced up and down her nerve endings. He pulled away so he could look into her eyes. "Then we see where this goes, what it becomes. Because I've never felt like this, either." She nodded, entranced by his stare. His eyebrow lifted and his voice lowered. "But I promise if you hit me like that again, I'm going to put you over my knee and let you know what I do to people who act out."

She lifted an eyebrow. "Is that a challenge or a threat?"

"A promise." He waggled his eyebrows before he put the car into drive and pulled back out onto the road.

"The maps and the information Alpha was getting us should be on the island by now," Charley spoke as she stuck her arm out of the car again.

"Yeah, either someone from Sierra Team will make contact or Reaper will bring it by."

"Not Phoenix?"

Smoke shrugged. "He's probably still around. Not sure if they are going to haul his ass back to the States or not."

"Why would they?"

"Shadows are supposed to go through Go/No Go evaluations prior to being in the field."

"But he's not really in the field, is he?"

"Technically, doing a job that requires him to be a Shadow? No. But for Shadows, the pressures are different. Taking a life takes a toll, no matter how seasoned or jaded you are. None of us are psychopaths or sociopaths. We are monitored to make sure what we do doesn't become more than we can handle."

"What happens if it does?"

Smoke shrugged again. "I don't know. I'm assuming medical intervention and repurposing."

"The Shadows in the program at the Rose were few and far between." She'd assumed two others beside Smoke were Shadows. She knew of Smoke before she went to the Rose because of her connections, but the two she believed to be Shadows at the Rose were… intense. Like Reaper and Phoenix. One left the program, but the other was paired up with an operative. They seemed to get along well enough.

"Because to do the job they do, you have to have a certain mentality. Most Shadows don't like anyone to know who they are or what they look like."

"But Reaper and Phoenix had no problem with me knowing."

"Because I'm your partner. Make no mistake, both of them are extremely lethal. Don't ever forget that, Charley. In my role, I support just about every Shadow Guardian utilizes. I know what they look like, and their codenames, and for most of them their specialty, but that's it.

Knowing any more gets you killed because then you become a liability to them and to their job."

"They wouldn't take out a Guardian." She scoffed at his warning.

"True, but they'd never fuck up and tell you more than they could afford to tell you. They're professionals."

"Unlike the asshats we're tracking." She grabbed at her hair that had dried enough now to fly away in the breeze from the open windows.

"Which will be their downfall. Disabling the sub won't take much. A small charge to the rudder and propeller will disable it without killing whoever is still inside."

"Then the four of us and Sierra team start hunting." She leaned back in the seat.

"If they don't go on the offensive first," he agreed.

"Which they very well may do. They went after me when they had the chance."

Smoke sighed, "Ever ask yourself why?"

"Because they thought I was following them, which I was."

"Why didn't they just slit your throat and walk away?" Smoke glanced over at her. "That's not out of the realm of options, so ask yourself the question: why didn't they?"

Her mind went to the obvious, but there was no way they could know anything about her background. Finally, she admitted, "I don't know. Do you?"

He tipped his head from side to side. "Actually, I think it could be that they weren't authorized to do so. If this guy is echoing what he saw at the very beginning of his indoctrination in Guardian, he would have been modeling it after the strict compliance phase. When I was brought in, I couldn't shit without permission."

She nodded. That first three-month period was about following orders and testing your integrity. "So, they are foot soldiers that don't think on their own?"

"Or are afraid to do so. The man and woman you spoke with, did they give any indication they could make decisions?"

"I think the woman was strange. I meant to ask Reaper this morning, but there is something off about her. She was… hell, I don't know, but she rang every warning bell I had. He was a handbag for her, you know what I mean? He was a prop."

"What was different about her?"

She sighed and tapped her hand on the frame of the door. "I can't really place what was different. She was just too... extra, you know what I mean?"

"Extra?"

"Yeah, over the top, extreme. Almost—" She turned suddenly. "Shit, Smoke, I need to see a picture of Clayborne."

"On my phone. In the emails. "He nodded toward the cupholder where his phone sat. She held it up to his face to open it and then scrolled through to his email and pulled up the picture. "Oh, man. He's a fucking genius."

"What?"

"He's hiding in plain sight."

Smoke whipped his head toward her. "What are you talking about?"

"I think he's disguised as a she."

"Okay, so, how do we validate your assumptions?"

"Has Reaper seen this?"

"I don't know. Call him. Number three on the speed dial."

She pushed the speed dial and put it on speaker as Smoke entered Georgetown traffic. She watched as he tugged his cap down further over his face and put his hand up in the window, blocking sideways glances.

The phone rang twice before it engaged. She glanced at Smoke, who chuckled, "Hey, asshole, did you get the picture Alpha sent?"

"Hold on," Reaper answered. He came back on a few moments later. "Nope. No pictures."

"Hold on." Charley echoed his words. She went to the email, downloaded the picture onto the phone, and then sent it via text. "Check your text messages."

"Well, that's interesting. Is this who I think it is?"

"Yes. The one and only."

"Different nowadays."

"I agree. We'll contact the powers that be and inform them of our suspicions."

"Roger. Anything else?"

"Nope." Charley laughed. "In a hurry to get rid of us?"

There was silence for a minute before he responded, "I don't know how to answer that, so I'm not going to."

The call ended abruptly, and Smoke looked at her. "Told yah, a different breed."

"Indeed." She glanced up after clearing the

phone. They were close to the hotel. "We unload our supplies and then get ahold of Guardian."

"Sounds like a plan. Then food, sex, and sleep."

She sighed, "In that order, please."

"Your wish is my command, my dear."

She snorted, "My dear?"

"Meh, better than Bambi."

Charley groaned and mumbled, "I'm going to murder Phoenix."

CHAPTER 15

Smoke carefully unwrapped the first of many items they'd rescued from a watery grave. Seeing his ship scuttled sucked, but the silver frame she'd retrieved for him was probably the only thing that couldn't have been replaced. Demos gave it to him with a picture of the obliterated group home in it. He could remember the man's words as if they were spoken yesterday, his New York accent ringing clearly in his mind.

"When you find a memory that brings you more satisfaction than this one, you put it in here. Until then, remember the injustices that happened to cause you to

do this. That's what we're going to rectify, boyo. One monster at a time."

"Alpha online."

"CCS online."

"Annex online."

"The Rose, and this better be good, some of us actually work for a living," Fury sighed into the phone.

Charley glanced at him and took a reinforcing breath. "Does Clayborne have a sister?"

She heard typing as Jewell answered, "I'm on it. Here is his folio, hold on. Family… nope."

"Okay, well, then I believe the picture you sent of Clayborne is actually now the woman who tried to intercept me the other day."

"Repeat that. No wait, explain that. I heard you, but I don't understand," Alpha corrected himself.

"I think he's disguising himself to move freely." Charley stared at the phone intently. Smoke moved over and placed a hand on her shoulder. She jumped slightly and lifted her hand to cover his.

"Jewell, we should have pictures by now from

Sierra Team. Run a comparison. Now," Alpha's voice snapped the command.

"Already on it, don't get snippy, Bubba."

Charley covered her mouth with her other hand, and Smoke bit his lip to prevent himself from laughing.

Joseph had no problem laughing at Jewell's reprimand and encouraging her. "Get after him, Button."

"Did you make your dive?" Anubis stopped the family squabble before Jacob could retort.

"Yes. We recovered enough to do what we need," Smoke acknowledged and winked at Charley, who raised her eyebrows. They'd recovered enough to sink the fucking island.

"Good. You should be receiving the information soon; the courier arrived about thirty minutes ago. We'll need a date and time frame of when you're in play. The method is up to you. And be careful. Those subs can hold more than just the players we're watching," Alpha cautioned him.

"Copy all." The exact number of players on the island was a question mark.

"The facial recognition program identified three potential matches to the photograph. Clayborne is one of them."

"What does that mean to us?" He needed to know because taking out the wrong person was not in his game plan, although Reaper and Phoenix were probably going to be given the green light for that portion of the operation.

"Facial recognition can and will bring in false negatives and positives every now and then. Clayborne's not a perfect match, and that could be due to the shading or angle of the picture."

"So, we take her and her companions," Fury interjected.

"And if Clayborne and this woman just happen to look alike? Doppelgangers exist," Anubis cautioned.

"We could alert them. Hell, for all we know, this woman could have been modified to look like Clayborne to cause just this type of confusion," Jacob concurred.

"So, what's the game plan?" Fury volleyed the question immediately.

Smoke spoke up, wedging his way back into the conversation. "I don't know why this changes anything. We disable the sub as planned. Keep our ears on Camelia and Renaldo and watch. If this is a disguise, Clayborne may break his cover to either kill or meet with Renaldo."

Charley agreed. "At that point, you activate whatever asset is the best fit to flush Clayborne out of hiding and take action."

"And what happens if he doesn't make a move?" Jacob countered.

"Then we give him something he wants," Anubis answered.

Fury sighed, "Which is?"

Charley cocked her head. "Me. They've made a play for me once already."

Anubis cleared his throat and spoke hesitantly, "Yes, but we have another who they are contracted to eliminate."

"Unacceptable on both points," Jacob snapped.

Fury added, "But if necessary, possible."

"It might not get to that point, Alpha, but if it does, we have plays," Anubis agreed.

"Why do they want Charley, and didn't we change her codename to Bambi?" Jewell asked.

"God, no, please don't bring the codename thing up again. Bambi. All I see is a cartoon deer and a bunny thumping the ground. So not a code-name. But as to the why, I was the only one they clearly saw on the ship. Smoke stayed to the shad-ows, so they don't know what he looks like. I assume they want to know what agency is following them." She looked up at him and shrugged.

Jacob took over the conversation. "All right. Stick to the plan. Smoke, give me a date and approximate time for your op. I'll brief Archangel. We wait and watch while we disable the sub. Alpha out."

"CCS out."

"Do you need anything from either the Annex or the Rose?" Fury inquired.

"Negative," both he and Charley responded at the same time.

"Perfect. Anubis, stay on the line, we'll discuss the other options just in case."

"Affirmative."

"Then we're out." Charley ended the call and sighed. "Alpha was quick to veto me being involved."

He moved back over to the supplies and motioned for her to come over and help. "I think Alpha was quick to nix both options."

"Do you know who the second person they may be interested in is?" Charley used her Interceptor 911 to slice through the outer wrapping of a brick of C4.

He nodded. Tempest. The man had taken out

all of the Fates, and Akuma was their fucked-up insurance policy. He worked with Sierra Team, so he was on the island.

They worked in silence until all the exterior wrapping was off their bounty. To remove it from sight, they stacked it under the sink in the bathroom. His det cord was waterproofed along with the C4. The directional blasting caps they'd have to re-wrap, but they could do that with common materials they could buy on the island.

A sharp knock on the door sounded. He had his weapon drawn, and when he looked so did Charley. He motioned to her to take the corner of the room diagonal from the entrance. He'd open the door and she'd cover.

She nodded when she was in place and he reached over and opened the door. "Listen, asshole, I'm not coming in until you put down your fucking weapons."

Smoke chuckled and lowered his weapon. He opened the door and extended his hand. "Tempest, dude, we were just talking about you."

"All bad I assume?" Tempest strolled into the room. "Well, hello. Who are you?"

"Charley, Tempest. Tempest, Charley, my partner in all things."

Tempest's smirk told him he got the hidden meaning, but the man pointed at his own eyes and said, "Nice to meet you. Don't let him hit you in the face next time."

"Screw that. I wouldn't let him hit me at all." Charley crossed her arms and glared at Tempest.

"Spunky. She'll do." He reached into his shirt and pulled out a packet of papers. "This is for you."

Smoke took them and handed them over to Charley. With the exception of the map, they were useless to him unless he had hours to work through the pages that would take others only minutes to read and understand. "Thanks."

"So, why are we babysitting the dickwads at the hotel?"

Charley stopped unfolding the paper and looked up. "Didn't Guardian brief you?"

"Of course, they did. But..." Tempest nodded toward the plastic and tape scattered all over the floor by the bed. "That's wrapping from your goodie selection. Any excitement we need to know about?"

"Nah, man. Far away from you."

Tempest grunted. "Good. I'm liking the calmer life these days."

"How's the wife?"

"Perfect. Sorry to hear about Sage."

Smoke nodded. "He's got a handful of shit at home. He'll be back."

Tempest's gaze slid from him to Charley and his eyebrow rose in question. "She's my partner. If he comes back, we'll worry about it then."

"No worries, actually." Charley looked up from the papers. "Nothing wrong with three people on a team."

"Huh. Sounds like you are making management decisions, Spunky."

Her head lifted and she leveled a gaze on Tempest. "What is it with you Shadows and nicknames?"

Tempest laughed. "Why?"

"Phoenix calls her Bambi." Smoke ducked out of Charley's reach.

"Oh, I like Bambi better. Those big brown eyes. Yeah, I can see that." He clasped Smoke on the shoulder and headed to the door. "See you later, my friend. Bambi." He pulled the door closed just in time to avoid a shoe hitting the wood panel. His laughter from outside the door was easy to hear.

"You just had to tell him, didn't you?" He ducked as the other shoe sailed over his head.

"Hey, now, remember what I told you." He

lifted a hand as she stalked toward him, and albeit laughter was impeding his reaction time, he was able to slip away from her when she made a move to clock his arm again.

"Yeah, well you deserve it. Why would you do that?"

She feinted to the right and he lunged, moving behind her and pinning her back to his chest. He didn't want to hurt her ribs, so he grabbed her hips and held her against him. "Settle down, you little hellion."

She placed her hands over his. "Why? I got you where I wanted you." She turned her head so she could see him. She pushed back slightly and smiled. "Right where I want you."

"Hmmm, I thought we were supposed to eat first." He tipped his head and kissed her. When she moved, he released her and then cradled her in his arms as she turned around.

"Oh, I'm going to eat." She pulled at his t-shirt and he took the hint, ripping it off in about three seconds flat. She smiled and reached for his board shorts, unfastening them. "We need to take a shower."

"Are you sure you're up for that?" He stepped out of his shorts as they dropped to the floor.

"The way I want you, yes." She stepped away from him and dropped her shorts, leaving her shirt and swimsuit still on. As she backed away, the rest of her clothes followed gravity's pull, and by the time they made it to the bathroom, there was nothing but skin between them. He reached in and turned on the water and helped her into the tub. He stepped in and pulled the shower curtain behind them.

The feel of her silky skin as the warm water cascaded over them rekindled the insatiable intensity that consumed him every time they were together. He soaped his hands and carefully traveled her body as they kissed. Time was irrelevant. The only time that mattered was this fractured piece, away from the harsh reality of their lives. Her hands mapped his body with the same reverent slowness with which he memorized hers. If tomorrow never arrived, the time between them would be the pinnacle of his existence. Love was a foreign concept until recently. Until now.

Charley broke the string of kisses by turning around and bracing herself against the front shower wall. She gazed at him over her shoulder and bit her lip. He ran his hands up and down her back before he positioned himself behind her. He moved forward, slowly and carefully. Tonight wasn't about power or speed. Tonight, he would tell her with his body what he would most certainly fuck up if he tried to speak the words. He was shit with those kinds of things, but this… this he knew. Distracting her with soft kisses to her back, he worked her tight nipples with one hand, always making sure to hold her so there were no sudden moves that would jar her ribs. He withdrew and moved forward, each time entering her a bit further until he was seated deep inside her. Was it her trembling or was it him? He didn't know because, fuck, they were perfect together. He wrapped one arm around and slipped his hand between her breasts before his palm cupped her neck. He held her hip with the other and moved in and out of her, adjusting how he moved to ease her ribs.

"So damn good." Her words floated on the fog-like mist the hot cascading water created in the confines of the small shower. He couldn't agree more. They were so damn good together. She surrendered her weight to him, trusting him to take care of her. Charley wasn't a trusting person, with good reason. Her letting go in moments like this nourished him in ways he didn't understand, but he knew he needed her, needed this connection, and never wanted the way he felt right now to end.

Charley's hands slipped from the wall, but he held her, cradling her as he drove them both farther up that cliff. He lifted her a bit and kissed her shoulder. Her fingers weaved through his hair and she turned her head. They kissed in a sloppy sideways fashion. It didn't matter. The need to be connected in as many ways as possible seemed to dominate her thoughts, too. He felt her muscles tremble and soaked in her small gasp as her sex tightened. He followed right behind her, bracing one arm on the front wall of the shower, keeping them both upright.

When he slipped from her, she stood up, forcing him to straighten. She turned and wrapped her arms around his waist. Placing her head on his chest, she whispered, "Charley isn't my name."

"I know."

"I can't tell you what it is. Not yet."

He dropped a kiss on her wet hair. "That's okay."

"I will. One day. I'll tell you." She lifted her head.

He bracketed her face in his hands. "You have a good reason for hiding who you really are?"

She nodded. "But I've shown you who I am, this is me. You know more about who I really am than any other person."

"When you can, help me understand. Until then, we have this, and it's more than enough to sustain us."

Her stomach rumbled loudly in argument. Her eyes widened before she dropped her head to his chest and started laughing. He chuckled and turned off the water. "I think your stomach is disagreeing with me."

"Well, we haven't eaten today." She looked up at him, those big brown eyes luminescent. "I think I may be in danger of that emotional attachment I told you I wasn't going to form."

He bent down and kissed her. "I think we both are in uncharted waters. I feel it, too."

"You taught me how to do everything underwater. Maybe we should just sink into the uncharted waters and let our instinct take over."

"I already have." He leaned down and kissed her again. They hadn't said the words, but he knew that someday, they would. When that time would come was anyone's guess, but he'd wait.

CHAPTER 16

Smoke watched the small motel and carefully scanned the area. Charley had stayed in the hovel while he went to gather the supplies they'd need and made a stop at the small diner where he'd eaten with Reaper and Phoenix. He took a photo of the specials board and menu and sent them to Charley. She called him and read them to him. He ordered and came back to the hotel, although by an alternate route. At one point, he'd picked up a tail. The little jaunt around Georgetown was enough to verify he'd lost them, but he wasn't in a hurry to lead anyone back to Charley, so he parked a block over and watched.

Overkill? No. He'd learned to trust his instincts.

Someone had been following him earlier. That

white van lingered too long before it turned after him. The angry driver stuck behind the van honked, drawing his attention to it. Then the driver sped through a traffic light to keep from losing him. He slowed. The van slowed. He sped up, and the van followed suit. He could see two people in the vehicle, but why would they be trailing him? Were they rabid Chris Collins fans or someone less innocent?

He made the decision to lose them and speed dialed Charley as soon as he could.

"What's taking so long? I'm starving, remember?"

"Picked up a tail."

"Description?"

He rattled off all the information he had on the van. "Call Reaper and let him know. I'll make sure I shake this asshole before I come back. Take care of yourself."

"Only if you agree to do the same. Don't you fuck up and get dead."

"Awww… is that concern I hear?" He gunned the engine and flew through an intersection, leaving the van buried behind two cars at a red light.

"Maybe. Maybe more than that, but you'll never find out if you don't watch your ass."

"Such a sweet talker."

"Always. Seriously, be careful."

"Will do. Call Reaper and make sure you have your weapon close."

"What, you're not going to tell me to lock the door?"

"Nah, figured if I treated you like a two-year-old, you'd hit me again."

"You know, for a career bachelor, you're learning fast."

"Hey, I can be taught. Gotta go." He ended the call, glanced in his rearview mirror, and took a sharp right and then an immediate left. There were no vehicles behind him, so he stopped and backed into a small driveway behind a low row of shops. He was in a perfect position to see anyone coming or going, but seeing him would be difficult, especially as night was rapidly falling on the small island.

His phone vibrated beside him. He answered it without looking at the caller ID. He knew who it was. "What do you need?" Reaper growled the question.

"Send Phoenix to the hotel. She's not one of us.

She'd take out a few of them, but she'd be in trouble."

"Do you want her to know?"

He snorted, "Do you want me dead? Hell no, don't tell her I sent backup. She's pretty damn proud of being self-sufficient. Tell Phoenix to make some shit up."

"Pride will get her killed," Reaper warned.

"Not if I'm there to keep her safe. Give me an hour. I want to make sure these assholes are gone before I head back."

"No worries. We're fucking bored to tears. I don't know how the regular operatives do this shit. I don't like it."

"It takes some getting used to," he agreed. Before he transitioned to a Thorn team, he'd receive a location to meet the Shadow who he supported. They'd let him know what needed to be done. The constant coordination and top-down direction chafed his ass when he first started working with a partner, but he'd adapted.

Reaper grumbled, "With any luck, this is the one and only time I'm playing James Bond."

"Hey, Bond was an assassin."

"Bond was a minion of a political puppet master like all the alphabet bitches."

"Why don't you tell me how you really feel?"

Reaper huffed, "Just did. Watch your ass. Whatever it takes."

"As long as it takes."

Now, he didn't see or feel anything off. Several people left and an older couple entered the office and came back out only to unload their rental and drag themselves into their room, bickering the entire way. He glanced at his watch. Nothing in over an hour. He lifted from his position in the darkness and moved forward with his supplies and their dinner, careful to keep to the darkest parts of the building. At the door, he knocked. The door opened and he slipped in, locking it behind him.

He nodded at Phoenix who'd opened the door and at the small table where Charley had obviously been looking over the charts. "Did you buy enough for three?" Phoenix smiled at him.

"Still have an appetite?"

"It would appear."

"Then yes." He'd only gotten two meals, but he'd fucking give his food to Phoenix if the man could keep it down.

"Awesome." He lifted away and grabbed the bag. "I'll warm it up."

Charley stood and stretched. She looked at

Phoenix and then at him before she shook her head. “Didn't think I could take care of myself?”

Phoenix chuckled. “She saw through me showing up in like two seconds.”

Smoke shrugged. “Sorry, not sorry.”

Charley leaned up and kissed him. “Okay, the ribs are still sore. I'm not going to bitch too much.”

Phoenix laughed. “That’s not true. She bitched the entire time you were gone.”

Charley shot Phoenix the finger and he laughed again. They split the food and Phoenix left shortly after they finished eating. Charley tossed the takeout containers into the wastebasket and motioned for him to join her on the bed. She pulled a map of Grand Cayman out of the stack and ran her fingers along the latitude and longitude lines. “Here is where they believe the sub is located.”

He grabbed the navigational charts from the stack of paper and lined it up with the map she'd used. With painstaking care, he studied the bathymetry maps indicating the depth of the water in the location the sub was resting.

“There, that's how they got so close to the east side of the island.” He traced his finger along the ridge and the natural inlet that formed due east of the small cove the lat and long triangulated on.

"I see. That is a narrow channel. Whoever navigated it was good."

"That's the way we're going to go in." He tapped the elevated area and ran his finger to the nearest place they could enter the water without being seen—or be seen and not noticed.

Charley squinted at her map. "That's a public beach, and look, it has a dive site. Ten bucks says there are cruise ship tours out to the site."

"That's perfect. We'll slip in and make our way out through this area and into the sheltered cove through the channel here. We rig the sub, blow our charges to disable it, and swim out the same way we came in."

"Should we blow the access point on the way out? That would ensure the sub doesn't leave." Charley glanced up at him. "I don't want to damage the reef, but it would be a foolproof way of keeping them stranded should the charges not work the way we want them to or if the damage isn't as extensive as we want. We're balancing on a thin rail. Alpha wants it disabled, not damaged to the point of destruction."

He examined the channel. "We'll make a game-time call. Right now, I think I can disable it by taking out the propeller and the upper and lower rudder plus the exterior lift planes. If we get it right it is a tube with no ability to go in any direction. Those parts aren't something you can go to the corner market to replace."

"Okay, when do we go?"

He stared at the maps again. "The sooner the better. Tomorrow morning."

"Which means we have a late night of building charges and making them watertight." Charley picked up the maps and folded them as she spoke.

"Five charges. Small enough not to breach the hull of the sub but large enough to fuck up the propulsion and steering."

"Don't forget the charges for the reef. Game-time decision means being prepared to make the call and blow the fucker. In order to do that, we need to build the charges." Charley went into the bathroom and came out with two bricks of C4.

"The consideration would be how to crumble the reef without blowing us up, too."

Charley sat down on the bed and deposited the explosives. "I know you don't like them, but I think we should use timers on these charges." She held up a hand. "We can disable the charges as we swim out and bring them home. Set the timer for way longer than we would take to disable the sub, which would give us a cushion. If we don't need them, we're golden. If we do, the reef tumbles into the channel and we make our way back to our car, the sub is taken care of. A failsafe."

He didn't like working with timers, hated it as a matter of fact, but there were times when they had to be used, and this was one of them. "All right. I agree. Making sure that sub doesn't leave with Clayborne is paramount. Let's get started."

Smoke woke to a thousand pins stabbing his arm. He opened one eye. Charley was laying on his arm. Damn, the fucker had gone to sleep and was waking up in an extremely obnoxious way. He clenched his fingers together several times, setting the needlework to jackhammer mode. He shifted and Charley rolled. The blast of blood to his appendage sent pinpricks of sensation flooding through his arm. Not pleasant. He glanced at the clock and closed his eyes again, trying to decipher the numbers that jumbled in his brain. He lifted his head and glanced at the door. No sunlight coming around the edges or from the one and only window they had. He closed his eyes and rolled over, tucking Charley closer to him. They'd gone over every move they'd make several times. She was an excellent diver and her skills with explosives were growing. They'd swim in, place the charges, and swim out, deactivating and taking the reef charges with them.

He'd run the possible pinch points in the operation over and over. They'd discussed what could go wrong and what to do if it did. How to handle a compromised charge or det cord that failed. What to do if the sub's propeller was thicker than the information they'd been given. They agreed on sign language over hand signals to eliminate any questions during communication. He closed his eyes and took a deep breath. They'd prepared for everything. A thread of apprehension snaked up his spine. He'd had the feeling before. The sense of foreboding weighed heavily as he ran the plan over and over. His gut told him something bad was on the horizon. He knew it just like he knew the sun would rise in the morning. The bitch was that there was nothing he could do except run the plan again. *Fuck.* He started at the beginning…

CHAPTER 17

"Do you see anything?" Smoke asked as he took yet another turn, taking them away from the place they wanted to be.

"No. I think we lost them." She gazed out in the other direction. There were storm clouds on the horizon, and that wasn't figurative. The massive front was blowing up from the south. If they didn't get into the water soon, they might not be able to complete the dive. Lightning didn't strike the water as often as it struck land, but water was a conductor—and if they were near the surface, they'd be toast.

"There is a storm coming in."

"Check on your phone and see how long we have." Smoke picked his way through traffic and headed back toward the east side of the island. "Maybe we're just paranoid."

She snorted. "We are paranoid, but that SUV was pretty sketchy."

"How did they find us? I checked the car for tag devices." Smoke's eyes kept darting to the rearview mirror.

She pulled up the weather app and hit the radar. "Time-lapse gives us two hours before the storm is on top of us."

"That means an hour and a half. I want to be out of the water thirty minutes before that storm reaches us." He accelerated and merged into traffic which was littered with cruise ship busses and a plethora of taxis shuttling their tourist fares this way and that. As they traveled east, traffic cleared a bit.

They parked at the far corner of the public access dock and suited up. Her new Interceptor 911 was strapped to her calf as was Smoke's. They carried their supplies down to the beach while wearing everything for their dive but their flippers. She sat down and put hers on while Smoke did the same. They high-stepped it into the ocean and lowered into the surf. The process of wetting her mask and putting it on took less time than the last dive. Her nose wasn't as sore, and although her black eyes were wicked, she felt pretty good. As long as she didn't overextend, her ribs were staying a discomfort in the background instead of being an attention-grabbing pain in the... well, ribs.

She glanced back toward the beach as she treaded water and rinsed her mask. “Fuck, Smoke.” She nodded toward the beach as she slipped on her mask. The SUV that had been following them was parked beside their rental and two men were searching the lot.

“Let's go.”

She nodded and put her respirator in her mouth, checking the flow once again before she deflated her belt and sunk under the water. The shroud of water pushed against her and the comfort of routine settled around her.

Smoke gave her a thumbs-up and she returned the signal. He started out first and she fell into a quick but comfortable pace next to him. Using her legs as primary propulsion, she managed to keep her ribs from screaming too much. The water was a pristine blue and clear to the point of being eerie. The rippling streams of sunlight cutting through the mass of the water from the surface added to the otherworldly effect of the dive. Horse-eye jack fish flashed in brilliant symmetry as they switched directions in perfect unison. As they neared the reef, she spotted angelfish and a school of blue tang that looked like darker dimples along the reef until they moved. When they neared the inlet, a massive school of silverside fish darted away, moving in an undulating frenzy that shifted like smoke through the current.

They inspected the protrusions of coral and placed the charges that would crack the ancient habitat, blocking the exit. She prayed the explosions wouldn't be needed. Destroying something of this beauty would be a heinous crime. The alternative, though—letting Clayborne escape—wasn't an option, either. She mounted her charge and glanced over at Smoke. He lifted a finger, then two, and they both clicked their timers when they hit three. They had two hours. If all went well, it would take twenty minutes and they'd swim out and disable the charges.

She kicked a bit harder to catch up with her partner. The camouflage netting was easy to spot under the water. The fact that it had been tied in place with rods driven into the ground indicated they were here with professional divers or they'd been here before and the area was used regularly.

Smoke turned to her and made the sign for danger or threat, a motion that resembled him blocking a knife coming at him. He did it twice. She glanced at where he pointed. The sub had sensors deployed.

She signed back, ***You work, I'll swim in and out. Fish***. Just like the lesson he'd taught her on his ship about fish swimming in and out of sensors and humans not doing it.

He held out his hand for the supplies she had in the bags tied to her belt. Then he signed, ***In together. Out together***.

She gave him a thumbs-up and they moved to swim next to each other. He grabbed her and swam into the sensors and down the length of the submarine. He released her at the propeller, and she swam out of the sensors, doubled back, and maneuvered through the sectors, swimming back to the front.

As she curved around, she stopped. Four divers were heading toward the sub and Smoke had his back to them. She slid her knife from its scabbard and pounded on the hull of the sub.

Smoke's head snapped up and she signed danger and pointed. He turned and she raced toward the incoming divers. They were fixed on

Smoke, who went back to work. She slid her knife home and started swimming toward Smoke. Two of the divers saw her and branched off.

She changed direction and headed toward the netting. Glancing back to make sure the fuckers were following her, she twisted violently, just missing being skewered by a barb fired from a pneumatic speargun. Her ribs screamed in instant complaint, but she couldn't stop. The other had a speargun, too. She dove for the ocean floor. Reaching it, she scooped up an armful of sand and sediment and kicked with her fins as hard as she could, clouding the water around her before she sank down in a crouch and waited, palming her knife.

Another barb shot through the clouded water and she shoved down on her heels, launching through the muddied water. She collided with a diver and struck. Her knife glanced off a tank and hit the fucker's arm. She rolled and punched through the water again, landing the sharp-as-fuck knife in the man's chest. She pulled it out and twisted, but not before the other man's knife sliced her thigh. She pushed the first diver toward the other and dove. Blood clouded the water as well as the sand that they kicked up. She rolled and glanced behind her. The uninjured diver was on her. She twisted, but the diver grabbed her high-pressure hose and pulled, spinning her. Charley stabbed backward as the bastard sawed on her high-pressure hose. She nailed the fucker but lost the grip on her knife which now protruded from his leg.

The pop of the high-pressure hose releasing at three thousand psi was audible under the water. She twisted and found her attacker trying to swim away. The wound from her knife in his leg trailed a dark red wave behind him. She still had several minutes of air left due to the restricted orifices on the high-pressure line, but she needed to hurry.

She struck out to where she'd left Smoke. A small boat engine whined overhead. She glanced up and watched as three more divers split the water from above. There was a cloud of blood and debris around the rear of the submarine. She prayed hard and swam harder. She caught the motherfucker with her knife in his leg. It took less than a minute to retrieve it and slice the fucker's neck.

She glanced at her watch, which was the computer for her dive. The amount of air left was minimal, but she couldn't surface without knowing. As she started to move toward the rear of the sub, she was caught from behind. Something jerked her leg and she twisted and then gasped. A metal weight hit her head. It felt as if she staggered, almost as if she were on the surface, and then… nothing.

She woke in stages. The voices around her echoed loudly. She drifted for a moment until she heard the sound of a gun cocking. She opened her eyes and realized she was lying on a dock beside a pile of equipment. She scanned the feet and ankles of the people who were standing in front of her. All except one were pointed in the opposite direction. She snaked her hand out and waited. Nothing. The angry voices continued, and she looked up. Six men stood in a semi-circle around Smoke.

She had no idea what language they were speaking, but what they were saying was instantly understandable. Chris Collins' name was said several times. The divers were arguing amongst themselves as to whether or not the man in front of them was actually Chris Collins.

She used the distraction to search the pile of equipment. *There.* A loaded speargun. She shifted slightly while watching the group in front of her. They were intent on what they were doing. She knew Smoke could see her moving because he was standing, facing them. As she continued the slow slide up the mound of equipment, she froze. A handgun lay at the top of the pile. *Holy fuck.* She dropped her hand on the pistol and flipped the safety off.

A small click of metal against metal. A tiny noise, something that would barely register to normal humans, placed a cataclysmic course of events into motion.

Charley lifted to her knees as she unloaded the clip. Three were down before they could turn, the fourth managed to pull his weapon. The fifth leaped forward and to his right, saving his sorry ass, and the sixth…

The sixth shot Smoke.

His body bucked and he spun, dropping into the water. Time fractured. She felt her trigger squeeze as she killed the sixth. The fifth ran, screaming as he went. She lifted and staggered to the water. *Where did he go?* She started to drop into the water when she heard the sounds of more people running. Grabbing the sixth man's weapon, she lifted her arm and fired.

She took cover behind a large support post of the dock and stared out at the water. *Where was his body?* Wherever the tide had pulled it to, she couldn't reach him without making herself a target, but she'd seen the bullet strike him, she'd seen him spin and fall. A bolt of lightning flashed across the horizon and a low rumble of thunder reverberated, shaking the air around her.

Realization of indisputable facts settled around her like nuclear dust, deadly and silent.

The man she loved was gone, and her life, her fucking dreams, and her ambitious goals were the most inconsequential things on the face of the planet. She heard a shuffle of feet at the edge of the dock and drew a breath. She stared at the ocean and said goodbye to not only Smoke but also her grand plans.

With a certainty, Charley knew she was going to kill every one of the men coming for her—or die trying. She gathered her strength and pushed past her shock and grief and reached down deep, finding a bloodlust rage. Clinging to the emotion, she checked her weapon, lifted, spun, and opened fire.

CHAPTER 18

Reaper lifted from the white leather sofa where he was listening to inane prattle from the yacht across the bay. *No.* He flung the headphones off and vaulted from the yacht to the pier, running to the woman staggering toward him. He reached her just as she collapsed. He scooped her into his arms.

Phoenix was beside him in the next second. "Get their last known location from Guardian and find him."

The man didn't waste time. His phone was in his hand and he was running toward the parking lot. Reaper carried Charley onto the boat and into the main cabin, shielding her from prying eyes. The blood on her wetsuit was dried and flaking off. He unzipped the damn thing and peeled it off her carefully. A bullet wound to the shoulder and a nasty-looking knife slice on her thigh were the only injuries he could see. He bolted to their field kit and started gathering supplies as his phone vibrated in his pocket. Well, fuck them, he had priorities. He poured alcohol on a sterile pad and tucked it in the knife wound. The bullet was still in her shoulder; as a matter of fact, he could see it just under the skin. Either the fucker had bounced around and splintered or had splintered and then hit her. He used alcohol to clean the tweezers he was using and moved the wound opening to assess what damage he could see. It was minor. Thank God. He fished around and finally grasped the shard of bullet, pulling it out with minimal fuss and very little bleeding.

Staring at her wetsuit, he'd have almost guaranteed she'd been hurt worse. The grey suit was burgundy-brown with blood.

He packed the small hole in her shoulder with gauze and only then did he grab his phone.

"Status," Anubis immediately snapped the command.

"She has a knife wound to the thigh that will need stitches and she's lost blood, but I have that under control. Looks like a ricochet piece of a bullet to her shoulder. It didn't go deep. I pulled the shard and have that packed.

Anubis asked, "Is she conscious?"

"No."

"Wake her up," the growl came from Fury.

"Hold on."

Reaper fished around in the medical kit and found what he was looking for. He popped a capsule of ammonium carbonate and shoved it under Charley's nose, making sure to keep the correct distance so he didn't burn her skin. The woman jerked, moaned, and then gasped. "Smoke!"

"What happened?" Reaper asked, the phone lying beside them so whoever was listening could hear.

Charley stared at Reaper. She pushed herself up and he dropped a couple pillows behind her to help her sit. Her body shook violated by grief. Her voice echoed her gut wrenching feeling of loss, "I searched for him. I looked everywhere. He... there was nothing except the blood off the pier. Oh, God, Smoke's dead."

Reaper stopped fussing with the damn pillows and sat down. “Tell me.”

It was as if she were recounting a story she'd heard a long time ago. Her heart was screaming in pain, but those feelings were sealed away by a molten hatred of herself and the fuckers who stole Smoke from her.

Charley detailed the swim to the inlet and placing the timed explosives on the inlet to keep the sub from leaving. She moved on to the sensors and then the divers.

“What happened then?”

“I was knocked unconscious. The next thing I know, I was waking up on the pier. No one was watching me. I saw a chance and I took it. That's when Smoke was shot. I killed him.”

“Did you shoot him?” Reaper's cold, deadly tone forced her to lift her eyes from the knife wound she'd been fixed on.

“No.”

“Then you didn't kill him. He knew what the dangers were with this assignment. What happened then?”

“The storm was moving in, but I heard them coming for me. I killed four with the weapon I took off a dead body, one with a knife, and I broke another's neck." She shook her head. "I couldn't find him. After, I mean. I looked. God, I looked until the rain made it impossible to search further."

"No body?"

She shook her head. She searched until the explosions at the reef detonated, which would bring people. She stole a car from the several that were parked at the secluded area and drove to the one place she knew there'd be help.

"Then there's a chance."

"Of what? I saw them shoot him. I searched!" She stared at Reaper, who lifted an eyebrow.

He picked up the phone that was lying beside them and put the thing on speaker. "Did you get that?"

Anubis' voice rang out loud and clear. "Affirmative. Phoenix will report in. Do you need a doctor?"

Charley glanced at her leg and her shoulder. She rolled the shoulder and winced but didn't make a sound. "Give me some medical-grade superglue and I'm fine."

"We have it." Reaper lifted away and headed to the medical bag.

"How many people did you take out?" Fury asked.

Charley pushed her hair away from her face. She growled the words, "Every last fucking one of them."

"We need to pull you in," Archangel entered the conversation.

"Bullshit. I just put a major fucking dent in those supposed assassins of Clayborne's. They took down my partner and I want to see that asshole and his fucking minions dead."

"Charley, I'm not going to argue about this—"

"Fucking perfect, Jason, because neither am I. You don't want me out in the field anymore? You want me out of the organization? You've never been comfortable with me working for you. Not a fucking problem. You give me this. You give me the chance to take this fucker down, to avenge my partner, and I will walk away. You'll never see me again."

"Charley, that's——"

"Do we have a deal or not? Because if you say no, I'm going after the motherfucker myself, and you know I will do it, with or without you." She damn near screamed at the phone.

"Jason, perhaps we should talk." Fury's comment ripped through the sudden silence.

"We'll call you back. Reaper, keep her there."

"Affirmative," Reaper said as he handed her the superglue.

She took the tube and dropped back on the pillows.

He removed the packing from her thigh and pressed the skin together. She leaned forward, took the tube out of the metal cylinder it was in, and opened the top before she dispensed the glue to the cut he held together.

As he held her thigh, he asked, "How much do you know about Smoke? I mean, as a Shadow Operative?"

She drew a shaky breath. "Other than he's primarily a supportive player, not much."

Reaper chuckled. "Support? Yeah, that's Smoke selling himself short again. That maniac fought his way into the middle of the fucking desert to save my ass when a mission went sideways. He hid me and fucking nursed me back to health before he went out and acquired comms to contact Guardian and send in the cavalry."

She leaned back and stared at him. "He never told me that."

"He wouldn't. He's not that type. There are more instances, but they aren't my stories to tell. He and Demos watch over us. Demos stopped coming out to the field—he's allowed to slow down and retire; the man could be my grandfather —but Smoke hasn't. He isn't a support role, he's essential, at least to us."

"But he's been floating around the ocean with me for the last four months."

"Because he's training you. After he and Sage went through training at the Rose, they'd show up together if they were needed. Shadows are singular by nature, but we aren't the old breed. Support and tech are necessary, isolationism isn't in our DNA like it was in the previous generation. Do we work independently? Absolutely. Are we lone wolves like our predecessors? Not necessarily."

"He won't be coming to help this time." She closed her eyes when Reaper withdrew his hand. The slice in her leg held together.

He placed butterfly bandages across the sealed cut to reinforce the glue's bond. He spoke as he worked, "That's where I think you're wrong. If you didn't see a body, I'm not willing to count that man out. He's one of the most intelligent people I know, even if he can't read."

She shot her questioning gaze at the huge assassin.

"We all know. Doesn't mean shit to any of us.

He's earned our respect. Now, how are you thinking of engaging with Clayborne?"

She clenched her shaking hands together. "Call them and set up a meet."

"Just call them, huh? You think that will work?"

"It will. They don't know I'm Guardian. They don't know I have support on the island."

"And they'll pick an area where they have the advantage."

"Of course." She drew a deep breath. "I saw the man I love shot today. Unlike you, I don't think he could have survived. I will kill Clayborne, and if I die, I die."

"A suicide mission? Not a smart play, Bambi."

"The only play we have is me."

"There is another."

"No, the other person has a life, maybe a family. I've estranged myself from my family and just lost the man I love. I am the right choice."

"Emotion blurs one's vision." Reaper shrugged.

"How do you know? Have you lost someone?"

"Not by death, but by my choices." Reaper's voice quieted.

Charley shook her head. "What?"

He lifted off the bed and shoved his hands into his cotton slacks. "The person I care about doesn't know. I couldn't bring myself to tell them."

"What's stopping you now?"

"Distance and time."

She stared at him a bit before she shook her head and sighed, "It isn't a bullet and a watery grave. Make it right."

He swallowed hard. "Perspective has a way of slapping a person in the face, doesn't it?"

"Too true."

The phone rang and Reaper moved over to open it. He put it on speaker and dropped it to the bed. "Phoenix is on-scene. Unfortunately, so is almost every Grand Cayman police officer and the local news. He is lurking until he can get in safely to look for Smoke. Jewell has tapped into the coroner's computer system, and as the bodies are brought in and photographed, we'll have an accurate accounting of the situation," Archangel spoke without preface.

"And?"

"Our plan. You're in, but you are under our command."

She closed her eyes and relaxed her shoulders.

"We know where the woman is staying."

"But we aren't sure that woman is Clayborne.

We need positive identification. This organization will not subvert its values, no matter the cost. Do you understand me?" Jason growled the words.

"I hear you loud and clear," Charley acknowledged. Her mind was on revenge and only revenge.

"Reaper, when Phoenix returns, both of you will leave the island. Phoenix returns here and your mission brief will be waiting for you when you touch down."

Reaper turned and looked at the phone. "Sir?"

"We have Sierra Team in place, this will be a tactical mission, and keeping eyes on one person without the proper team training will be hard enough. Phoenix is to return for his Go/No Go, and you are needed elsewhere."

Reaper's eyes swept over to hers. She nodded. She got it. He wanted to avenge his friend, too. "I'll take them down." She whispered the words.

"I copy all, sir." His tone let their handlers know he wasn't happy.

"Sierra Team will make contact with the plan of attack. And Charley, those men you took out weren't Akuma's elite. They were ROK regular army."

"How do you know that?"

Jewell cleared her throat. "There may have been a back door into some databases."

"No, I mean how do you know they aren't Akuma?" She winced as she got out of the bed.

Jewell explained, "The type of people we are hunting have no past, no records to trace back to a native country, and definitely no records for random hackers to find through backdoors in shitty government computer systems."

She looked over at Reaper, and he nodded his head in agreement. "Do we know where Clayborne and his elite are located?"

"We have a damn good idea. Sierra Team has developed some intel. They'll make contact once the op is confirmed."

A scream from outside snapped both of their heads up. Reaper launched out of the cabin and grabbed a pair of binoculars. "Guardian, stand by."

Charley limped out to stand by Reaper. "What's happening?"

"Look."

He handed her the binoculars, went back into the cabin, and apprised Guardian of what he'd seen. She lifted the glasses and focused in. A man floated face-down in the water as a woman screamed by the railing of the Honduran Yacht.

"Fuck. Renaldo." She moved back inside and listened as Reaper reported what she'd assumed, too.

"There was no talk of a meeting," Jewell spoke quickly after Reaper finished.

Fury grunted, "Then Clayborne has found another meal ticket or way into what is left of Stratus."

"Or Renaldo was his target all along," Reaper spoke. "Renaldo was wanted for crimes against the Crown in Spain. They could have taken out a contract."

"On it," Jewell interjected.

Anubis spoke, "They'll be moving soon. If Renaldo was his mission, they'll be moving out."

"The sub is a no-go. We clogged the inlet," Charley reminded them.

"Do they know that?" Fury asked.

"I don't know. I neutralized everyone that showed their face. There could have been someone I didn't see."

"They have to know about the divers finding you."

"I don't know. Maybe. I didn't see anyone talking on a phone, but it could have happened when I was out." Charley rubbed her head. "It seemed like these guys were posted there. It felt like they were guarding the area to keep any tourists or locals out of the cove to make sure they protected their exit strategy."

"How would they know you were there?" Anubis asked.

"Air bubbles." It was the obvious answer. Someone had been charged with watching the water around the sub. If they were looking with binoculars, their release from the regulators could be seen.

"It could still be their exit strategy," Reaper agreed.

"Jewell, are the police and the news agencies still at the scene?" Archangel probed his sister.

"Checking with Phoenix. Stand by."

"It will be an open crime scene for a long time," Charley mused quietly to Reaper. He nodded. "They'll try to find a way to get to the sub."

He shrugged. "If I were them, I'd hold up and wait for the heat to recede." Reaper rubbed his chin. "Best case, they do, and Sierra Team can track them. Then we go in with the team in the lead and take them all down."

"We don't have positive ID on Clayborne," Archangel added himself to their conversation.

"So, how do you suggest we get positive ID?" Fury growled.

"Let me talk to whoever it is. I can play the deranged girlfriend."

"And you'll end up with a bullet in your brain. No thanks," Archangel snorted. "We take them down, but there is no more body count added. I realize you did what you had to do to make it out of the situation you were in, but we've captured primaries before. Sierra Team is well versed in extraction scenarios. We go in, extract as many as possible, and let Jared's interrogators take over." Archangel's tone left zero room for disagreeing with his decree.

"According to Phoenix, they are bringing in generators and tents are being set up. They're in it for the long haul. He doesn't think anything could get within a mile of that lagoon without the Grand Cayman police knowing about it."

Anubis asked, "So, we go after them where they've held up?"

"The hotel." Charley was surprised. That was going to be a mess. Too many civilians in the area.

Archangel disagreed. "No. They've moved. The phones stayed in the hotel, but the people moved. Sierra Team has the location."

“Sir, a request,” Reaper spoke when it appeared the conversation was about to end.

“What?” Archangel's tone didn't soften, but he seemed receptive.

“I'd like to stay for the op, sir. I think Smoke would have wanted me to make sure someone had Charley's back. I'll do that and keep her off Sierra Team's scope so they can maneuver without worrying about her. Unless my next assignment is time-sensitive, I can finish here and shove off within the next twenty-four hours.”

There was a long pause before Archangel spoke again. “Request approved. Archangel out.”

CHAPTER 19

Charley shrugged off the pain in her shoulder. Tomorrow morning, the injury could be tended to by a professional, or she'd be dead and it wouldn't really matter. She leaned on the side of a building about five clicks from where Sierra Team had an overwatch on Akuma's new hideout. They'd gone over the exterior of the house, thanks to pictures taken by the overwatch. The problem was the interior of the home.

Sierra Team's Leader—Travis, as he was introduced—was hunkered down with a stick not more than four feet away from her. He tossed a couple rocks out of the way and drew a rough outline of the house. "Here is the structure. It's big and it has three levels. According to Harley's pictures, there are two smaller outbuildings, both with locks on the outside and no visible signs of movement. I don't give a flying fuck. Luke, you and Scuba clear them and be damn quiet about it. When you rejoin, we'll breach here at the back of the structure." He pointed with his stick to the roughly drawn door. "Ricco, you have entry and Harley will have your back. I'll brief him when we get to his position."

"Roger that, Skipper," the man she assumed was Ricco answered immediately.

"Scuba is in third, break right. I'm in next with Coach and Luke on my six. Coach and Luke are responsible for our fallback and backflush. No surprises. Just like we trained. We sweep right. When we've cleared the area, our guests come in and we move as one. One team, one movement. I'll give the go. Nobody moves without my order."

Charley watched as all eyes shifted to one of the men. The guy rolled his eyes and groaned, "Geeze, one time, three years ago. For God's sake, let it go, will ya?"

The team laughed and Travis winked at the man he singled out. Charley chuckled too. The relief of pressure was probably a good thing.

"Equipment check, keep your shit tight, and stay safe, I'm not leaving fucking paradise without each and every one of you assholes." Travis dismissed his men and came over to where she and Reaper were waiting.

"Not sure what your purpose is on this op, but we clear, then you enter. Stay out of Luke and Coach's way. If they say get down or move, you follow orders, copy?" Travis shifted the sling of his M-4 to his other shoulder as he talked.

Reaper nodded. "We won't be a hindrance."

"That's right. Because I won't let you be." Travis smiled and winked at Reaper before he moved over to his team.

"You sure you want to be a part of this?" Reaper asked again.

She turned and stared at him. "I won't be left behind."

He indicated the men with a tip of his head. "These teams are highly specialized and trained. They can almost read each other's minds. If they give you an order, follow it. If we fuck up, it could cost one of their lives."

"I've lost more than enough already." She whispered the words. "I'll stay tight."

He stared at her for a moment. "Then let's check our gear. We don't want to be the ones to cause those fuckers to know we're coming."

Charley cocked her head at him. "You already checked your gear. I watched you."

He snorted. "Fine. Check your fucking gear, Bambi. Make sure you're soundproof."

She lifted an eyebrow. "I have, but I'll do it again." The check gave her something to do while she waited. Her reality slapped her in the face. This was her last operation. Smoke was gone and everything she'd worked so damn hard for was scattered like broken shards of glass around her feet. Perhaps it was for the best. She closed her eyes and shook her head. No, nothing about this situation was for the best. It all sucked. Every single iota.

Travis stood and gave a low whistle. His men lifted and fell into formation around Reaper and her, and they moved as one as quietly as possible through the tropical underbrush that would lead them to the old building where Clayborne was reported to be. She wanted to look in that man's eyes and promise him the time he'd spent in jail was a cakewalk compared to what Guardian was going to provide him. *Bullshit.* She wanted to put a bullet between the man's eyes, and that rage was one of the real reasons she'd walk away from her dreams.

The stoic deliberateness of her movements and

her actions would end when this mission was finished. She'd find a corner and cry until there were no more tears. She'd mourn the loss of a love that she'd only just found. When the pain let her, she'd find something to do with her life. Something impactful with a legacy, other than the one she'd sought recently. She skirted a downed limb and earned herself a nod from one of the team members. They pushed through some low brush and Travis raised his hand. They all went to a knee and she sucked in her breath as she felt the slice on her thigh pull tight. The seeping wetness along her leg told her it had opened again. That too would have to wait.

A man lifted out of the underbrush and ghosted up to Travis. They spoke for several seconds before he took his place in the formation and they moved forward on Travis' hand signal. As they approached the small clearing to the east of the building, Travis planted them again. With hand signals, he dispatched two of his men. She lost track of them about two hundred meters up the path. They stayed still and waited. About four minutes later, the two returned and had a brief conversation with Travis. The man turned around and stared at her. She could read the indecision in his gaze. A chill ran down her spine. She moved forward. "I will not hold you up. Reaper is here if you need to move fast." She could feel the assassin behind her.

Travis nodded and gave the hand signal to rally. His men converged seconds later. "There's an unknown player or players involved. At one of the outbuildings, a man was found nearly decapitated. We don't know if this is one of their own dispensing punishment or if we are coming in after another entity. All eyes open. Full comms are up, but don't talk unless it's absolutely necessary, leave the channel open for me."

She nodded as did all of his men.

Travis made eye contact with each of them. "All right then, let's go."

They crept forward and lowered into a crouch as they moved around the building. Travis sent several of his men ahead and they waited. He rallied them again, moving back to where she and Reaper were holding to stay out of sight. "Another down. Neck broken. This has all the signs of a mission going to shit. I don't know who or how many are ahead of us and I don't need the two of you to worry about."

"Then don't," Reaper said. He leveled his gaze on Tempest. "Tell them."

"He's in my old line of work." Tempest whispered the words.

Travis pinned Reaper with a stare. "That's awesome but not helping me in a tactical environment. I'm going to have to trust you to keep her ass out of the fire. My direction from HQ was emphatic. She is to be protected at all costs."

She narrowed her eyes and hissed, "*She* is right here, and *she* took down at least ten people this morning when her partner was shot and killed in front of her. I'll take care of myself; you worry about your team."

Travis' eyes bored into hers. She wasn't going to flinch or give a fraction of an inch. Getting to Clayborne, identifying the motherfucker, and then being the one to put a bullet through his brain was her goal, and she would be the one. She'd earned that fucking right.

Finally, he nodded and diverted his gaze to his team. "Same plan, but we're going in hot. We have at least one person in that building who isn't taking prisoners. Be smart and do this by the numbers. We train for a reason. This is it."

The men nodded and they moved as a group to the edge of the brush. Travis sent two men first. When they slid into the shadows of the building, he motioned Reaper, Charley, and another of his men forward. She slipped into the shadows and moved silently to where the others had migrated. The last three men followed, and the team moved soundlessly into a line. All of them placed their hand on the shoulder of the man in front of them. When Travis dipped they all did, and then they moved forward.

She watched as they deployed as one. Many moving parts, one seamless sequential action. When motioned, they moved up. She slid right as she'd seen the team do with Reaper behind her. The pool of blood she stepped over had come from the body propped in a half-sitting position against the wall. His head listed and hung from his shoulder, tethered by only the skin and muscle of the right side of his neck.

Reaper pointed to a smudge on the floor. A portion of a bloody footprint. She tapped Travis on the shoulder. He spun and glared at her. She pointed to the smudge and then to the next one as they moved up to the stairwell.

Travis nodded. She watched as he directed one of his men to wait at the stairs while they cleared the rest of the building. Reaper pulled her to the side. "We'll wait here. If Clayborne is in there, they'll let us know." He whispered the words right before a bounding thud sounded in the stairwell. Travis' man watched with his weapon pointed at the narrow door leading to the stairwell. Through their comms, she heard his hushed, "Movement. Stairwell. Secure."

There was no response, but she didn't expect one. Even though making sure the building was secure before they moved up was the right move, the delay in getting to Clayborne grated on the raw nerves the last twenty-four hours had exposed. Her gut told her the bastard was upstairs on higher ground, but running in and getting herself killed before she took out the son of a bitch wasn't going to happen. She would end his life the way his men had ended Smoke's.

When the team reappeared, they moved to the second floor. There wasn't anything to indicate what had caused the sound in the stairwell and she and Reaper held in waiting with the same team member guarding the stairwell. She held her sidearm with her finger on the trigger guard, muzzle down, and resting against her leg. Closing her eyes, she could picture where Travis' team was by the sound of the men entering and leaving the rooms they cleared. The muffled sounds of soft steps would crystalize a bit before muffling again. The soft rubber soles of the combat boots they wore kept them almost silent.

When they returned, they moved quietly up the stairs, turning to mount the last flight, and found another dead body. The man's neck had been broken, and she'd take odds it wasn't from a fall. They moved forward, and this time she and Reaper trailed with the team. The sounds of pounding footsteps froze everyone in a defensive posture until the sound of a metal door slamming down the hall drew her eyes up.

The roof.

She motioned to Reaper, who nodded. "We have the roof. You clear the floor."

"Wait!" Travis hissed, but she was done with waiting. They sprinted down the hallway, past three more dead bodies, and up to a metal door. She took one side; Reaper took the other. He opened and she went low, he went high.

They cleared the small area and made their way up a set of four stairs to the roof. The door, ajar and moving in the breeze, swung out as Reaper pushed it. She peeked out and then rolled. With her weapon leveled, she cleared to the left side of the door as Reaper moved out, clearing to the right. She glanced at him and he motioned to her left and lifted three fingers. As he counted down, she drew a deep breath and slipped around the corner on a crouch, her weapon aimed and safety off.

No!

Reaper fired, his shot echoing hers. The executioner's head exploded, and he fell. She watched as a ghost jumped to his feet, his hands tied behind his back.

Smoke rushed Clayborne. They collided and hit the brick ledge on top of the wall and went over.

She screamed. Reaper's gun discharged, and out of the corner of her eye, she saw a woman spin and fall. Charley sprinted to the wall and skittered to a stop at the edge. "Smoke!"

Smoke looked at her from a lower level of the roof, his knee pressed into Clayborne's neck. Charley smacked her hand onto the brick and vaulted over the lip, yells from behind her be damned. She landed, properly splitting open the wound on her leg. She ran to him and grabbed her interceptor from its sheath. She sliced through the ropes binding his arms.

Smoke lifted up, hauling Clayborne with him. Smoke's hands went around the man's neck. "Tell me, motherfucker!"

"Smoke, don't kill him!" She grabbed his arm. Fuck, she never thought she'd say those words, but they needed to ID the bastard first.

Smoke's muscles clenched, keeping Clayborne on his toes and struggling to breathe. "Tell me and live."

"Tell you what?" she asked as she saw Reaper in her peripheral when he dropped down.

"Where is it located, you bastard?"

She had no idea why Smoke was acting like a crazed maniac. "Where's what, Smoke? Tell me what you want him to say because he's going to die if you don't give him some air." The man's face turned from dark red to purple and spittle hung from his lips as he tried to breathe.

"Tell me, motherfucker!" Clayborne's hands fell from Smoke's forearms when he passed out.

She pushed in front of him. "Don't kill him or you'll never find out." She wasn't getting through. Finally, she screamed, "Dan! Stop it!"

He blinked and looked down at her. "Charley?"

"Yeah, it's me. Stop choking him." She put her

hand on his cheek when his eyes went back to the nearly dead man in his hands. "Please."

The unconscious body dropped in a heap to the rooftop. He grabbed her and pulled her into him. "I thought you were dead," he whispered. "The police and all the body bags… I thought I lost you."

"I saw them shoot you." She reached down and put her hand over the bullet hole in his wetsuit. He put his hand over hers just below his armpit. A furrow creased the wetsuit, digging a trench in the outside of his arm.

"Yeah, it hurts like a motherfucker, too." He pulled her closer and dropped his head against hers. "I remember falling and I hit my head. I woke up in shallow water under the pier but thought you were gone. I couldn't… I had to catch the bastard. I couldn't…"

"I know. That's why I'm here. Sierra team is mopping up your trail." Or at least she assumed that was what they were doing because she didn't see them anywhere. Reaper had appeared and was now handcuffing Clayborne.

"The woman. She's his partner."

"Partner? How do you know?"

"They were fucking stroking each other's egos

when I took out their last guard," he sighed. "She shot Renaldo."

"How did you end up here?"

"I followed the bastard they sent to watch the scene. When he got into his car, I encouraged him to be cooperative."

"How?"

"I cut off one of his balls. Motivational as hell." His head snapped back to Clayborne. "They deployed their assassins before they came to the island. I don't know the missions, but one of them has directions to go to D.C. They mentioned a name."

Charley lifted away from him and stared up into his eyes. "Whose?"

"Clayborne told the woman that he wouldn't want to be Mrs. King now."

"Fuck." The word echoed from every team member who was now on the rooftop.

Smoke turned around and his eyes landed on Travis. "We need secure comms, now."

Travis pivoted and snapped, "Ricco."

"On it." The man hit a knee and started unpacking his backpack.

Smoke looked at Coach. "Is the woman dead?"

"Bleeding, but not dead," Coach muttered as he

moved forward with a medical kit. "The only one who is still alive, I might add. Well, besides that poor bastard. You racked up a body count tonight, didn't you?" He pointed at Clayborne. "Let me look at the two of you while we wait for comms."

"I'm fine."

They spoke the same words at the same time and then looked at each other. "You're not." Again, the same words at the same time.

"Holy fuck, someone hit them both over the head at the same time, didn't they?" Reaper rolled his shoulders. "Smoke, you got this. I have to haul ass to an assignment. Later."

"You know where I am if you need me," Smoke said as Reaper reached up, grabbed the lip of the higher roofline, and pulled himself up. He twisted and sat on the brick before he nodded. "Whatever it takes."

"As long as it takes." The words echoed eerily as the reply was said in unison by every Guardian on the rooftop.

Charley tucked herself under Smoke's chin and held him, letting a tiny bit of emotion leak from her closed eyelids.

"I thought you were gone," he muttered in her hair.

"I thought the same." She looked up at him. "You can't scare me like that again."

"Ditto." He lowered for a brief, soft kiss.

"Hate to break up the reunion, but we have a connection." Tempest dropped a hand on Smoke's shoulder.

Smoke nodded and they hobbled over to the radio. Travis authenticated and handed the mic to her lover.

It took every ounce of training he had to take the microphone. All he wanted to do was get patched up and crawl into bed with Charley for the rest of his natural life, but the stakes were too high now. Too high to wish for a rest and way too damn high to worry about anything but relaying the information he alone knew.

"This is Smoke."

There was silence before Fury came online. "Thank God. How are you, my brother?"

"Battered. I must have hit my head when the bullet knocked me off the pier. Thank God, I woke up under the pier and not at the bottom of the ocean."

Anubis agreed and added, "Glad to have you back, my friend."

Charley squeezed his hand and he glanced at her before he squeezed back.

"Start from the top, and I'm glad you made it." Archangel's voice held sincere warmth.

"Thank you, sir. But before I do, you, Joseph, Jacob, and Justin need to increase security on your wives."

"Explain." The warmth was gone in an instant.

"As I made my way to Clayborne I took out his guards. The last one was in the next room. I heard him and the woman he was with congratulating each other. He congratulated her on taking the shot that took out Renaldo, and she congratulated him on the deployment of his assassins. One, in particular, was heading to D.C. Clayborne laughed and told the woman that he wouldn't want to be Mrs. King. Her death was going to be particularly painful."

Jacob growled, "Motherfucker. Alpha out."

"I'm not in D.C., but fuck if I'm taking a chance. The Rose is out." Fury cleared the line.

"Stand by." Archangel checked out of the conversation.

"Let's continue with the debrief." Anubis took over. "What else did you hear?"

Smoke sighed. "They are working with the faction in Cuba that we disrupted about three years ago during a joint Homeland mission. They were Stratus. Jared King knows the ties."

Anubis cleared his throat, "Why do you say that?"

"Because right before I entered, they toasted each other for the renewed effort to develop dirty bombs in Cuba." The 'duh' was implied, but he was too fucking tired and relieved to keep the snark from his response.

"Fuck."

"Exactly my reaction when they saw me and bolted. I chased them up to the roof, but they had a guard up there. He got the drop on me and they had me trussed and ready to be drilled when Charley and Reaper showed." He glanced at Sierra Team. "Thank you for having their backs."

Travis lifted an eyebrow. "No offense, but they don't listen to instructions, and I'd rather they didn't come back to play with us."

"If we'd have waited, he'd be dead," Charley threw the reminder into the conversation.

"Or you would have been." Travis shook his

head. "There is no excuse for going rogue on an op."

Smoke dropped his good arm over her shoulder as Coach worked on her leg. "No offense, but I'm damn glad she did."

Travis stared at him and then pointed a finger at Charley. "I'm not excusing it, but I'm pretty fucking happy you did, too. He's an all right guy."

"Can we get back to the debrief now?" Anubis asked.

"Roger," Smoke said with a chuckle.

"You have Clayborne?"

"Roger that, and the woman who could be his doppelganger," Travis answered. "Ten bucks they fucked with a lot of people."

"All right, Travis, you'll need to sweep up. Alpha is offline and probably will be for some time, so I'm directing you to make sure the locals don't find out about this op."

"Roger, I copy."

"I'll let Alpha know what I've directed. Smoke, what is your physical condition?"

"Bullet in his upper bicep and slightly unequal pupils. Concussion is my guess," Coach spoke up as he wrapped clean gauze around Charley's leg.

"Stand by." Anubis' voice cut through the argument he was going to launch into.

"Charley, you have incoming. Saint Priority. ETA thirty minutes. You will be at the ship Phoenix and Reaper were using in no less than twenty-nine minutes. Do you copy and understand?"

He flicked his gaze to the woman he thought he'd lost but never would again. She closed her eyes and shook her head but answered. "Affirmative. En route."

She opened her eyes and gave him a soft, sad smile. "It's time to face the music."

"I'm coming with you." He waved off Coach again as he followed her.

She stood up and limped over to the higher wall. Glancing back at the team, she whispered, "You don't have to do this. This is my reckoning, not yours."

A chill ran through his veins. "I refuse to lose you again. I'm coming."

She glanced up at the wall and then back at him. "Before we scale that brick, I'm going to tell you something. Something that will scare the fuck out of you, but I'm being honest for once in my life."

He braced himself. "I'm listening."

She glanced over at the team and then back at him before she leaned in and whispered, "I love you."

A flash of relief ghosted over him. "Good, because I love you, too." He knelt down. "Use my leg."

She stepped up onto his thigh and grabbed the top of the brick and with effort pulled herself up the wall. He jumped up, grabbed the top, and one-armed himself up far enough to slide over the brick.

The woman watched them as they walked past. Charley diverted and made her way to where she was tied. "Clayborne ratted you out. You're going down. Hard." Charley glanced over to the wall where Tempest was now sitting. The man gave her a two-finger salute, letting her know he'd play up the seed of doubt she planted.

Smoke put his arm around her, and together they walked past the dead bodies of the men he'd killed when he believed Clayborne had had his lover killed. He hadn't had any plan other than making the man pay. The intel he'd been able to gain was fortunate, and for the Kings absolutely essential, but he'd have killed the bastard if he never muttered a word. Then he would have found a ship and disappeared.

They used the vehicle the guard had driven him to the meeting place in. The blood on the driver's side seat didn't bother either one of them. They wiped out the car and left it three blocks from the pier. As the rays of the sun started to crest over the eastern horizon, the sound of a helicopter's blades beating the air pulled his eyes heavenward. A massive, shiny, black bird flew overhead, heading for the almost-deserted parking lot.

"Ah, damn." Charley turned to him. "This is the ship. Could you go into the cabin and grab a shower? I'll need a few minutes."

He stared at the crest on the tail of the helicopter. "Is that who I think it is?"

She looked over her shoulder and sighed. "Yeah."

Smoke stared at the tall figure in black battle dress uniform. "Why is he here?"

"I'll explain everything, Dan. I promise, but right now, I need to do this. Alone." She lifted up and kissed him in full view of the man striding down the pier. "Please."

He drew a finger down her jaw. "I'm here when you need me."

She nodded and grabbed his hand, holding it to her face for a second before she whispered, “Go.”

He glanced down the pier one last time and headed into the main cabin of the ship. Of all the people in the world to be striding down the pier. Who was Charley and why would…

He stopped in the middle of the cabin and turned around. “Oh, hell no.”

CHAPTER 20

Charley glanced down the pier, looking in the opposite direction from where the helicopter had landed. She didn't want to have this conversation within earshot of Smoke, so she turned and walked to the end of the pier and sat down. She was fucking exhausted, both mentally and physically. The adrenaline of hunting Clayborne, of finding Smoke alive, and the arrival of her long-awaited reckoning had carried her to this point, but fatigue and dread weighed down on her.

She leaned against the weathered wooden post and listened to the tread of his boots as he neared. She looked like shit. Two black eyes, dried blood caking her black BDU pants to her thigh, and a bloody piece of white gauze peeked out from her black tank top. Not the image she wanted to portray right now. When she imagined this meeting in her mind, sitting at the end of a wooden pier that smelled of boat fuel and stagnant seawater wasn't it, but it was time. She was tired of living a lie. This was her life, she should be able to choose how to live it.

He sat down next to her, and they remained quiet for several long minutes, their legs dangling off the end of the pier as they stared at a ship leaving the harbor. She didn't say a word simply because she didn't know where to start.

Finally, she glanced at him. The years had deepened the creases near his eyes and his hair had greyed some, but he was still the man she'd run to when life got hard. The man who'd saved her from her own stupidity when she was fourteen, and the man who'd loved her since the day she was born.

"Hi, Daddy." She leaned into him and he dropped an arm over her shoulder.

"Hey, Pumpkin. Looks like you've had a rough couple of days."

She chuffed a humorless laugh. He wasn't shocked, wasn't pissed, or even upset. He knew. She shook her head. "How long have you known?"

He drew a deep breath and released it slowly. "Since you approached Demos."

She jerked upright and whipped her head around to stare at him. "He *told* you?"

He reached up and grabbed her chin with his fingers, turning her face this way and that as he examined the bruising under her eyes. Finally, he released her chin and nodded. "Do you really think there is anything that goes on in my organization that I am not acutely aware of?"

She shrugged. "I'd hoped. So, you allowed this. All of this? The last two years of training and..." She spread her arms, indicating everything. Her words deserted her. All the planning, the goals she'd imagined for herself. How many had been reached because of her father's knowledge?

"You did it yourself. I didn't interfere."

"Right. You didn't have anything to say about the bullshit ops that Smoke and I have been sent on."

"No. That was all Jason. For some reason, you being hurt under his watch was unacceptable to him." He chuckled and dropped his arm over her shoulder again.

She bristled against the contact, but instead of jerking away, she crumbled. "Why not just tell me?

I've worked so damn hard to learn everything and to be a part of this organization."

"Do you want the honest answer or the Dad answer?"

"I think it's time for honesty all the way around, isn't it?" She drew a shaky breath.

"A clean slate would be an anomaly between us, wouldn't it?"

She nodded. "My fault."

He hummed. "Not entirely. My boundaries may have been too strict."

"You think?"

"It is my job to protect you. I didn't do that when…"

"Daddy, that was my fault. Entirely. I've accepted what happened was because I didn't listen. I felt invincible. I learned how vulnerable I was."

"You paid a price for youth's fearlessness that no one should ever pay."

"True, but if it hadn't happened…"

He glanced down at her. "If it hadn't have happened?"

She shrugged and looked out at the ocean. "I changed then."

"I know."

"I want to be involved in the organization, Dad. Hell, that's a lie. I want to be in a leadership role in the organization. I want to make sure the poison of the world doesn't infect those who can't fight off the corruption or the menace. I want to stand alongside you and brace hard against the type of evil that stripped my childhood from me. I need to be the one who makes sure monsters are extinguished and normal people don't have to fear walking down a street."

"And that is the reason you've gone through the trials and tribulations of the last two years."

She nodded. "I had to prove to you I could do it, and if I'm honest, I needed to know I could. Deacon and Ronan will slide into the organization when they finish their service. That's destiny. Gabby is happy living her life."

"But you weren't."

"Every time I brought up anything about the organization, you tuned out. *That's nothing to worry about, Pumpkin.*" She imitated him and then physically sagged. "Dad, I became an adult at the age of fourteen. I'm not a child, and I haven't been for a long damn time."

"I know, and it grieves me. I'm sorry."

"It's not your fault, Daddy."

He grunted and she chuckled.

"You're taking lessons from Uncle Frank?"

He shrugged. "Maybe. The girl who is in Paris?"

"Margo? She looks like me and she's super smart. Her passion is art restoration, but she couldn't afford the education or the internship. I could. So, in exchange for me paying the bills, she fools the protection team, and you get reports of what a good girl I'm being."

"You realize that alone would have had me worried."

She laughed and nodded against his shoulder. "Guardian Security is my future. I need you to let me in, Dad."

They sat silently and watched as the harbor awakened. Finally, her father sighed. "Two conditions." She sat up and looked at him. "First, you come out of the field. I'll bring you into the organization. You'll have to learn every section from the ground up, but not as an operative. You've proven your metal in that regard; no one is doubting your skills."

Images of yesterday flashed through her mind. "Jason does."

"No, he was amazed at your tenacity and grit. I, on the other hand, was not. You are your mother's child, after all." He nudged her slightly and she smiled.

"She's going to blow her stack."

"Oh, yeah, and *that* is the second condition. You tell your mother what you've been doing. When you do, I'll be on the other side of the globe. In a fallout shelter. For the next decade or so."

She glanced around to make sure there was no one in the area. "Are you telling me the great and mighty David Xavier is afraid of his wife?"

"Excuse me? Have you met your mother? Of course, I'm afraid of her, but don't tell her I said that."

"Never, Daddy. That will be our little secret."

"The only secret we have from here on out, right?"

"Deal."

"Come on. Let's get you to the doctor and get those injuries taken care of." He stood up and offered her a hand.

She managed not to wince or groan as she lifted, but it was a near thing. The material of her pants pulled away from the scab on her leg again. She glanced at her shoulder which had stopped bleeding. "They're not that bad. Smoke was hurt worse."

Her father lifted a finger, pointed at her, and said, "Which is another thing I need to take care of."

"Dad…"

"Charlotte, I believe you're exceeding my grace and tolerance. You head to the helicopter and strap in. I'm having a word with my employee who is much too old for you."

She squared up on her father and tossed her ponytail off her shoulder. "I love him. Nonnegotiable."

"Who said anything about negotiating, Pumpkin? I'm planning on scaring the ever-loving fuck out of him." He smiled wide and waggled his eyebrows.

Charley shook her head. "Do you kiss my mom with that mouth? And don't mess with him too much."

"She's said worse a time or two, and I'm dealing with an assassin. I know how far to push." Her father dropped his arm over her shoulder, and they sauntered back up the pier. "I'll offer him a place in the organization where you can be together."

She stopped and looked up at him. "You know he's…"

"Chris Collins' brother. Yeah. Hard to miss."

"No, he has dyslexia, it would be difficult for him..."

Her father smiled down at her. "I know. He's one of my best assets. Making changes to accommodate his dyslexia isn't going to be a problem. Everyone in our company is utilized to their fullest potential. Even wayward, pumpkin-headed daughters who do things the hard way just to get her father's attention."

"Well, this pumpkin-head knew you wouldn't let her work with you unless she proved herself serious and capable." She turned and walked backward as she spoke. "Be nice."

He frowned and shook his head. "Not happening. This is a dad thing. Get your butt on that helicopter and do not touch any controls."

"Did you fly here? Can I fly back?"

Her father rolled his eyes. "The other three were so easy."

She rolled her eyes exactly the same way he did. "The other three have zero personality."

"Calm and responsible does not negate a personality, Charlotte. Don't touch the controls."

She saluted and turned around. A smile spread across her face as she headed to her father's helicopter.

~

Smoke sat on the white leather couch and watched as Gabriel, the founder of Guardian Security, gazed as Charley walked down the pier. There were so many questions and emotions jostling through his mind that he wanted to slam open the cabin door and scream for her to come back, but the man coming aboard now kept his ass glued to the seat.

When Gabriel slid the glass door open and stepped into the air-conditioned cabin of the small vessel, he looked angry. Well, that made two of them. "Where did you send Charley?"

Gabriel took a seat across from him and stared at him. "Charlotte is waiting in the helicopter."

"Excuse me? Did you say Charlotte?" Of all the names she could have had, that name did not suit her at all.

"Charlotte Jacqueline. She's always hated the name. We've called her Charley most of her life." The stare across the space wasn't exactly hostile, but it wasn't friendly either.

"She's your daughter."

"That she is. My youngest daughter."

"Shit."

“Exactly.”

“I didn't know.”

“No doubt. Charley has been on a self-imposed quest which, as you can guess, has been making my management more than a little nervous.”

“I thought she was a King.” Smoke rubbed the back of his neck. “Not that what her last name is would make a difference.” Once he got out of his own way and stopped running from her, that was. He looked up. “What quest?”

“About two-and-a-half years ago, she approached Demos, who'd retired, and asked him to sponsor her into the training program.”

“Demos went along with it?” He didn't see that coming. “He isn't the type of person to back hair-brained ideas.”

Gabriel raised his eyebrow and cocked his head. “I doubt Charlotte would agree that her plan was hair-brained.”

“Then we'd agree to disagree. Why in the hell would she risk her life as an operative with you as a father?”

Gabriel frowned. “She believed that I wouldn't allow her to work in the organization if she didn't prove herself.”

Smoke chuckled. “She was right, wasn't she?”

Gabriel dropped his head back and stared at the cabin's ceiling. "It would seem while I have progressive ideas in the majority of my life, when it came to my youngest daughter, I was overprotective and strict."

"Because of what happened in Rome."

Gabriel's head snapped up. "She talked to you about that?"

"We've both been completely honest and upfront, sir." Gabriel had to know about his limitations; it would be in his file.

"Rome was difficult for my wife and me. It ripped Charley's childhood from her, but that one lashed out at the world instead of curling in. Life was hers to be conquered. She would stop at nothing to prove she wasn't afraid of anything."

"That's the Charley I know." Smoke chuckled before he leveled his gaze on his boss' boss' boss. "We are more than partners, sir."

"I figured that out when I saw her kissing you. I can't say that I approve."

Smoke ducked his head. He could see why Gabriel didn't approve. He was an almost-illiterate assassin who did little more than support those around him. "I understand. Fair enough." He cleared his throat and glanced out at the shiny black helicopter sitting in the parking lot.

"So, you'll take care of things, then." Gabriel leaned forward.

He turned his eyes toward the man he'd respected most of his adult life. Hearing that he didn't measure up for his daughter hurt as if the truth was a dagger Gabriel had pushed through his heart. He rubbed the center of his chest and tried to breathe, willing himself to remain stoic in front of the man who founded the organization that saved him. "No sir, if you don't want your daughter around me then you'll have to tell her that yourself."

"I'm afraid you've misunderstood me. She's my daughter. Put a ring on her finger. Oh, and get a new ship. The two of you are not living with me." Gabriel stood and reached into his pocket. "This should work. Also, find and talk to Phoenix. While you're at it, get him to go see Doctor Wheeler. I'd hate to have to sideline him because of his eating issues."

Smoke took the paper and looked down. A smile formed and he nodded. "I'll talk to him sir, but he's not in a good place."

"That's why I'm asking you. You've helped raise

this class of assassins. Lycos has the babies, but Reaper, Phoenix, Valkyrie, Harbinger, Malice, Flack, and Ice know and trust you. Lycos' new group will need the same guidance. Charley wants to run Guardian someday and I believe that she and her brothers will eventually take over. In the meantime, work with me and Anubis. The Shadows need connection. We've learned that from your group. Trying to keep you apart, segregated and isolated, was a mistake. Be their connection, the tether that keeps them grounded." Gabriel put his hands on his hips and waited.

"I'm honored, but you realize I have… issues."

"Yeah, your damn brother."

Smoke barked out a laugh. "True, but that's not what I meant."

Gabriel lifted a hand. "I know, son. We'll make it work."

Smoke dipped his head. That was the first and only time someone had called him son. He cleared his throat and asked one final question. "Sage?"

A scowl crossed Gabriel's face. "I'll take care of him when and if he wants to come back. I'll make sure he has support, but I can't force him to return to us."

Smoke nodded and lifted the paper. "I'll take

care of this. Will you let her know what I'm doing?"

"Nope. I'm telling her you're on a mission and that you'll contact her. My sticking my nose into her life is something she fights tooth and nail. What she doesn't know won't hurt her. Serves the little miss right for scaring me to death yesterday."

"You and me both."

"Yeah, well we thought we lost you, too. All over a son of a bitch with delusions of grandeur."

Smoke looked at him. "Sir, didn't you hear?"

"I've been briefed. We've put up the fortress walls before. We'll do it again. Let those fuckers try to mess with one of our women. They have no idea the bombardment of agony and torment that will rage unfettered if they try. Get your wound tended to, get your shit together, and then come get Charley."

Smoke smiled widely and extended his hand. Gabriel grabbed it and pulled him in for a hug. As he backed away, Gabriel froze. "Fuck."

"What?" Smoke's gut froze.

"I just realized she's going to be in Virginia with me and her mother. Get a move on it, son. I can barely handle her mom, both of them are going to drive me to an early grave. I wonder if there are any missions on the other side of the globe."

Smoke laughed and looked out at the helicopter. The spotlights were illuminating and then turning off. Gabriel groaned and turned, leaving the sliding glass door open as he jogged off the ship. Smoke walked out onto the deck and waved at Charley, who he could see in one of the front seats. He laughed as Gabriel sprinted to the helicopter. "I'll get right on that, sir."

CHAPTER 21

Smoke's solo assignment, the one Gabriel handed him in Grand Cayman that he was able to decipher with time and effort, was to eliminate a man who made his fortune selling young men and women to the highest bidder. The number of sick fucks performing the service had multiplied ten-fold since Guardian had taken down the Russian Mafia. Where there was a void, there would always be someone to step up and fill the need. This bastard was rich, connected, and currently held ten young men and women on the yacht for his friends' use and sadistic entertainment. Unfortunately, the other fuckers who frequented the ship weren't coded, so Smoke was forced to manipulate an opportunity to take out his singular target.

Drago Franconia was a man without a country, although he originated somewhere in Europe as far as the intel Guardian had on the bastard indicated. The man was an animal that lurked in dark corners, catered to darker desires, and would commit any atrocity against the young people he stole off the streets for money. Smoke waited and watched for two weeks. The goons that surrounded Drago were hired meat. Bulky and made for show. Drago wasn't stupid, however. There was one who accompanied him that had training. The man watched everything, chastised the meat when they got lackadaisical, and kept Drago on a schedule. He didn't partake at the parties and kept his eyes on everything. To get to Drago, Mr. Right Hand needed to be distracted, at least for a short time. Smoke made one phone call and waited.

He saw Valkyrie as she entered the five-star hotel, exactly when she said she'd arrive. When she walked through the door, a bellman tripped over a suitcase because he was staring. Hell, everyone looked at the woman. She was striking. Her commanding demeanor alone would capture a person's attention. Add the thick, waist-length, platinum blonde hair, vivid blue eyes, and killer body, and she was a distraction waiting to happen.

He flicked his gaze to Drago's crew. Every eye was on Val. She stopped in the middle of the grand lobby and cast her gaze toward the exclusive lounge where Drago and his men were having a drink before they headed to the ship for another night of debauchery. Yesterday, Val accessed a dead drop he'd built with the mark's picture in it. She made eye contact with the target and gave him a slight smile before she headed to the elevators.

Drago's meat joked and prodded the man to follow. Drago laughed at Valkyrie's target and motioned for him to chase after her. And he did. Val glanced over her shoulder and smiled at the man as he approached her at the elevator. They'd make their way to the room that had been rented for this purpose. She'd drug the man and leave him to sleep off his erotic thoughts while Smoke neutralized the meat and eliminated Drago.

Tonight, he'd use the garrote.

He slipped onto the ship as the festivities for the evening reached a crescendo and hid in the shadows as the meat moved the inventory back to the cages that held them. Slipping behind the behemoths and drugging them was simple. The hard part was not killing the sick motherfuckers. It was a close thing. His sense of justice screamed for him to help out the human race, but he'd never freelance. He wasn't going to jeopardize his connection to Guardian or his future with Charley. No, the meat would live, but Drago would not.

He listened carefully before he exited the main cabin. Drago sat on a lounge chair and puffed on a cigar. Silently, he moved forward as he pulled his garrote from his belt. He wrapped his gloved right hand and then his left in the wire.

Smoke had been trained at taking a life in an up-close and personal manner. He'd done it four times before. Each monster that he eliminated gave those they brutalized a chance at life and kept other innocents from the same ending. He reached the chair and whipped the wire around Drago's neck. The cigar flew back as his victim jerked and then reached for the wire. Smoke didn't kill the man right away. No need to make a mess. "Get up!"

The man choked and sputtered but lifted as Smoke maneuvered around the chair. He tugged the bastard to the rail. Drago hissed and begged in almost soundless pleas. Smoke pushed him against the rail and jerked the garrote with both hands as hard as he could. The sluicing sound of muscle and cartilage being separated was interspersed with the rush of outward air as his windpipe severed. He pushed Drago forward and let go of the wire. The dead body hit the water.

Smoke made his way over to the deck hose and turned on the water. He washed down the side of the ship, removing the trail of blood from the man's severed arteries. Fortunately, all the blood was on the outside of the boat. He sprayed the side of the ship down and then dragged the meat out of the interior of the cabin and down to the private pier. Keeping his eyes open as he worked, he removed the gangway and let it drop into the water before he raced to the bridge and started the motors. Guardian had provided him a schematic of the ship weeks ago, so he was able to decipher the controls and memorize the function of each. He put the engines in reverse and maneuvered the ship out of the isolated cove. When he hit open ocean, he took a deep breath and made two calls. One to Guardian informing them that the target had been eliminated with no other casualties, and the next call went through to Val.

"Took you long enough." Her deep, throaty voice put a smile on his face.

"They partied. I had to get him alone."

"Shame you couldn't just blow them all up."

"Too many innocents on board."

"True. Do you need anything else from me?"

"No. I'm good. Thank you for the assist."

"Anytime. You'd be there for me."

"For as long as it takes." He answered her with every confidence, especially after the talk he and Gabriel had.

Valkyrie was silent for a moment. "Very few people actually mean what they say."

"I am one of the few."

"I know. Goodbye, my friend."

The line went dead, and he glanced at the compass and then double-checked it, making sure he comprehended what he was seeing. He corrected his course and pushed the throttle forward. Normally, he'd take out the ship after freeing the hostages. This time he took out the bastard and sailed away with the ship. His first port fifteen minutes up the coast was to release his cargo to the people Guardian had prepositioned, and the second much further north was to give Guardian access to the man's computers.

He remained docked as he worked to bring the ship up to Guardian's computer and electronics requirement, install sensors, and gut and refit the interior of the vessel. He didn't want anything of that bastard's to remain and taint his future.

Three months and seven days was a hell of a long time to be away from Charley. Yes, they'd talked damn near every night. When she texted him, it was pictures of her doing silly things. He kept every one of them. They talked of the future, of what she was doing for the company, and what she was learning. They'd had several video chats, two or three of which had turned into sexually gratifying moments for both of them. It wasn't enough for either of them, but he took Gabriel's demands seriously.

He reached into his loose white cotton slacks and pulled out a black velvet box. The four-carat ring he had thought of buying wasn't snuggled into the velvet. No, he glanced down at the thick woven gold and titanium band. Charley never struck him as a person who would want a massive diamond. So, instead, he had the jeweler intertwine her first initial and his. The D and C were rose gold, the rope that weaved through and around the initials was titanium.

He pocketed the ring and put on a black long-sleeve shirt, leaving it unbuttoned. Smoke dropped down from his newly christened yacht and slowly walked to the bow of the ship. The *Bambi* was registered in his name, thanks to Guardian's magic. He hadn't told Charley what he'd named the beauty, but it was fitting. This ship was sleeker, smaller, and more updated than his last one. The ship was now pristine, and he wanted to give her the perfect name. There wasn't really any other choice.

The wind blew his shirt open, and he slid on his mirrored navigators as he watched a limo pull up to the end of the private pier where he'd been told to dock. When she stepped out of the back of the car, he smiled so damn hard his cheeks hurt. Leave it to Charley. She saw him, whooped loudly, and sprinted down the pier. All he could see were her long, tan legs as she ran down the pier but in fact, she wore cut-offs, a pair of Chucks, and a yellow tank top. Her hair streamed behind her in the wind, and he laughed when she vaulted over neatly-stacked boxes instead of going around them.

She kept running, and when he realized she wasn't slowing down, he braced himself. Like a heat-seeking missile, she launched into his arms. The force of the collision sent him backward three steps and about a fraction of an inch from landing on his ass, but he didn't fucking care. Charley was in his arms and kissing him.

He grabbed her ass with one hand and her head with the other and held her as tight as he could against him. God, he'd missed her. Missed her laughter and singing, missed her constant questions and all her moods.

She dropped her legs and he bent over slightly to keep their kiss. The slide of her tongue against his and the grind of her hips over his was bliss in the most intense way. Finally, he had to breathe and lifted away.

She panted as she stared up at him. "Hi." Her smile stretched wide.

"Hi, babe." He turned and nodded to the ship. "Welcome home."

She glanced at the vessel and a furrow lanced her forehead. "Home?"

He nodded and stepped back, dropping to one

knee. Charley's eyes rounded and she shook her head.

Not quite sure what to make of that, he extracted the ring box and held it in his hand. "Charlotte, would you do me the honor of marrying me?"

She put one hand on her hip and the other over her mouth as she stared at the ring he'd designed.

He cleared his throat and her eyes popped to him. "You're kinda leaving me hanging here, babe."

She dropped her hand and held up a finger. "First, I hate that name."

He lifted an eyebrow. "That wasn't a no."

She lifted another finger. "Home?" She pointed to the ship. He nodded, not letting his gaze stray from hers. She swallowed hard. "You mean like forever?"

"That is my plan."

She nodded and glanced at the ship before she took the ring box out of his hand. She lifted the band out and stared at the intertwined initials. "Did you talk to my dad about this?"

"The ring or the question?" He was starting to think the proposal was misguided. Why in the hell would someone as young and beautiful as Charley want to hook up with him for the rest of her life?

She cleared her throat. “Ah… the ring.”

“No. I asked the jeweler to make it. But if you don't like it, I'll get you any ring you want.”

She shook her head and slid it on her left ring finger. “No, ahh… my mom… I mean, my father gave my mother a ring with his initials intertwined in it as a wedding band.” She held her hand out and then dropped her eyes to him. “Are you sure?”

“Am I sure?” He stood up and took her chin in his fingers. There were unshed tears building. “I've never been surer of anything in my life.”

A small tear bridged her bottom lash and trickled down her cheek. “You can't quit on me. Everyone says I'm difficult.”

“I don't think you’re difficult. I think you are enchanting and stubborn and independent, and I love all of you. The part that gets in bar fights, the part that will always veer away from whoever is leading, the part that sings show songs, and the part that will blow up a tower and be excited when you do it perfectly.”

She swiped at the tear and shrugged. “It was pretty perfect, huh?”

“It was. We should do that again. Now, are you going to answer me or keep me guessing?” He pulled her in and held her against him.

"Promise me you won't regret it?" She leaned into him, and that's when he noticed she was shaking.

"I'll never regret loving you, Charley. Never."

"Then I'll marry you." She lifted and he dipped down to kiss those perfect lips. She pulled back. "No take backs."

He laughed and shook his head. "I promise."

"Good. Now, does this new home of mine have a bedroom?"

"Several. Would you like a tour?"

She shook her head. "Tour? No. Just get me to a Goddamn bed." She jumped up and he grabbed her ass with both hands and walked them both onto the ship.

Her tongue and teeth tormented his chin, jaw, and ear. By the time he pushed through their cabin door, he wanted nothing more than to rip her clothes off and have her beneath him.

She dropped her legs and stepped back. The tank top and shoes were off in less than a second. Her movements ignited his. He stripped out of his shirt and kicked off his deck shoes and they both were naked less than fifteen seconds later. Her chest heaved as heavily as his. His eyes consumed her until he saw the scar on her shoulder. He dropped his eye to her thigh. The light pink scar ran in a six-inch slice over the muscle of her leg.

As if she was reading his thoughts, she spoke, "No. I would do it all over again. No regrets, no what-ifs." She planted a palm against his chest and pushed him backward toward the bed. "We'll do the sweet stuff later. It's been three months. Hard and fast now. Sweet later."

He nodded and dropped onto the bed; his hard, heavy cock bobbed as he fell. Charley waited until he'd lifted onto the middle of the bed before she straddled his hips and then held his shaft. His hands grasped her thighs and they both moaned when she lowered onto him. She lifted and moved down again. He tried not to thrust, but the fucking need was so intense that his hips bucked on their own accord. She gasped and dropped down, her hands planted on his shoulders, and she lowered to kiss him. He lifted his legs up, moving her forward so he could wrap his arms around her. His hips kicked forward, and he moved into her. They developed a rhythm, her lowering as he pushed up, but they never stopped kissing. He snaked his hands through her hair and held her tight. She broke the kiss moments before her body tightened around him. They chased each other into orgasmic bliss, the sensations and emotions too much for either of them to last long. He caught her as she collapsed on top of him.

As she laid recovering her breath, he stroked her hair with one hand and with the other arm held her belted to him. There was so much he wanted to say and yet nothing seemed to form on his lips.

"You're stuck with me now, Collins," she sighed and rolled off him. He turned toward her, and they shared a pillow while staring at each other.

"I'm okay with that, but I do have to ask: what is your last name?" He'd never heard Gabriel's.

She laughed. "I'll tell you, but you'll have to sign an NDA first."

He blinked at her and lifted onto his elbow. "You're serious."

Her laughter stopped and she nodded. "I'll tell you everything, but…"

"I'll sign. Of course, you'll have to tell me what it says." He shrugged. That really sucked, but he trusted her with his life; he'd trust her with his signature, too.

"We can do that, but we'll let an app I found read it to you just to make it all aboveboard. But let's do that tomorrow. Today I want to spend in bed, with you."

Smoke dipped down and kissed her gently. "No matter your secrets, you're safe with me."

She wrapped her arms around his neck and stared at him. "I've never felt safer. Make love to me, Dan."

He pushed her hair away from her face and smiled down at the woman he loved. The woman who loved him for who he was, not for who he looked like. The weight of the moment struck him. "You love me."

She narrowed her eyes for a moment before she replied, "I do. I love the man you are. The Guardian you've become. The friend you are to others and the man you fought to be. I do love you. Only you."

He blinked back the emotion of their connection before he lost it and leaned down to drop a kiss over her heart. He'd found the permanent image for that silver frame Demos had given him. It would contain a picture of this intriguing and beguiling woman. Forever.

Charley stood wrapped in a sheet at the back of the ship. Smoke was taking a shower, but she wanted to explore the parts of the ship she hadn't seen… so, all of it. It was smaller than his last ship but newer, and he'd made it into a three-bedroom home. A den with what she assumed were secure computer systems and comms, a media room with a projector and gaming systems, a kitchen that would make a world-class chef shit themselves, and the bar and living room area were made for entertaining. She trailed her hand along the polished chrome railing and carefully stepped down to the lower level. There was a dinghy and two jet skis plus an entire area dedicated to SCUBA gear. She opened the storage bins and smiled. His and her gear.

She turned and looked up. The smile fell from her lips. "Oh, hell no." She braced both hands on her hips. "The *Bambi?*"

She grabbed the sheet that she was wrapped in and lifted it up to her knees. "Smoke, you asshole! The *Bambi?*" She yelled the words as soon as she made it up the ladder and marched straight for the cabin. She would make him pay for that.

"Now, listen, I can explain!" Smoke's shout

came from the bedroom, but the sound of him running up the back stairs was easy to make out.

A laugh erupted from her as she hit the main cabin. "You can run, but you can't hide, Smoke! I have a lifetime to make you pay for this! *Bambi*? Are you freaking kidding me?" Happiness bubbled through her as she grabbed the top of the sheet and held on as she started to run. "When I find you, you'll be sorry!"

EPILOGUE

Reaper backed into the shadows and watched as Charley popped up from the lower deck. He saw the happiness radiating around her. A halo of contentment shone from somewhere inside her as certainly as he breathed. Tucking back farther into a dark corner of the ship, he listened to his friend and his woman laughing about the name of the ship. A sad smile lifted the corner of his lips.

He'd leave now and come back later. Perhaps not. The wounds he'd received during the last mission weren't healing, and he wasn't sure if he'd bother to go to a doctor. Melancholy rested on his shoulders and he gave into the weight. Perhaps it would be best if he didn't. Best for himself and for her.

He slipped off the vessel and made his way down the long, solitary pier. The security was damn good. He was better. He made sure to reengage the system as he left. At the parking lot, he looked right and then left.

Where the hell would he go now? He'd always searched out Smoke. The man was his touchstone, almost a father-figure, although there was only little over ten years difference between them. Reaper swayed slightly and made himself move.

Perhaps he'd go back one more time. See her again, just… because. He'd take the image of her; happy and unaware he was alive and then, if no one contacted him, perhaps he'd let the wounds do what they may. Upstate Pennsylvania wasn't that far. He could drive there. His feet moved toward the rental he'd procured. He always went back. He always checked on her. Watching Charley and Smoke had opened an old wound that no physician could treat and time had yet to heal. When he'd left his home all those years ago, he didn't know how hard it would be to stay away. Harmony wasn't his anymore. He severed that connection at that point in his life when he'd taken a nosedive so far down into the depths of revenge, he knew he couldn't contaminate her. Leaving her was his lasting act of love.

Reaper folded his body into the mid-sized SUV and pulled out, knowing where he was going, and yet he prayed he'd be called away before he arrived. Harmony deserved so much better than him. She should have a husband, a family, and friends. What she ended up doing was keeping a small farm running for her bastard cousin. Reaper growled in the back of his throat. If he had any indication that Harmony needed to be free from that son of a bitch, he'd break Quinton's neck and remove her from that hell hole.

He merged onto the interstate and headed north. God help him, he was going back again. The torment he put himself through every year or so was his personal form of hell. It needed to stop. One of these times, she'd see him. Then what would he do?

Reaper leaned to the side and winced. The infection gnawing through his side burned like a bitch, but he'd been hurt worse and survived. He set the cruise control and headed home. This time, he knew without a doubt it was the last time. It was finally time to let go.

Would you like to read Reaper's story? Click here!

The End

ALSO BY KRIS MICHAELS

Kings of the Guardian Series

Jacob: Kings of the Guardian Book 1

Joseph: Kings of the Guardian Book 2

Adam: Kings of the Guardian Book 3

Jason: Kings of the Guardian Book 4

Jared: Kings of the Guardian Book 5

Jasmine: Kings of the Guardian Book 6

Chief: The Kings of Guardian Book 7

Jewell: Kings of the Guardian Book 8

Jade: Kings of the Guardian Book 9

Justin: Kings of the Guardian Book 10

Christmas with the Kings

Drake: Kings of the Guardian Book 11

Dixon: Kings of the Guardian Book 12

Passages: The Kings of Guardian Book 13

Promises: The Kings of Guardian Book 14

A Backwater Blessing: A Kings of Guardian Crossover Novella

Montana Guardian: A Kings of Guardian Novella

Guardian Defenders Series

Gabriel

Maliki

John

Jeremiah

Guardian Security Shadow World

Anubis (Guardian Shadow World Book 1)

Asp (Guardian Shadow World Book 2)

Lycos (Guardian Shadow World Book 3)

Thanatos (Guardian Shadow World Book 4)

Tempest (Guardian Shadow World Book 5)

Smoke (Guardian Shadow World Book 6)

Reaper (Guardian Shadow World Book 7)

Hope City

Hope City - Brock

HOPE CITY - Brody- Book 3

Hope City - Ryker - Book 5

Hope City - Killian - Book 8

STAND ALONE NOVELS

SEAL Forever - Silver SEALs

A Heart's Desire - Stand Alone

Hot SEAL, Single Malt (SEALs in Paradise)

Hot SEAL, Savannah Nights (SEALs in Paradise)

ABOUT THE AUTHOR

USA Today and Amazon Bestselling Author, Kris Michaels is the alter ego of a happily married wife and mother. She writes romance, usually with characters from military and law enforcement backgrounds.